FALLING IN LOVE . . .

"I didn't attend the picnic to be insulted by you," the viscount said.

"Then why did you come?" Joanna's anger started to boil as she sensed that he had an ulterior motive, and an unpleasant one at that.

Finally, as they stepped out on the wobbly dock, he said, "Perhaps I wanted a chance to study the strategy of my adversary."

"I asked you not to come here again."

"I didn't want to ruin Toby's pleasure. He asked me to join the party."

She gave a dry laugh. "And I'm the Prince of Wales. No, whatever schemes you have in mind for me, Lord Perth, won't work."

"Don't trifle with me, Miss Warwick."

"Come on, Joanna. The boat wants to get away from me," Toby shouted. "Uncle Terence, please help her down."

"I suppose I'll have to lift you into the dinghy," the viscount said dourly.

"Don't you dare touch me!" Joanna swung around so that the long fringe of her parasol swept across his face.

The viscount took a startled step back and staggered onto a rotten plank. Before he had a chance to regain his balance, he toppled over the side of the dock and fell into the mud below . . .

Titles by Maria Greene from Jove

LADY IN DISGRACE
LOVER'S KNOT

JOVE BOOKS, NEW YORK

Author's Note

The phrase "Persian cat" was not in usage until 1824, but it was the best way to describe the feline duo, Penny and Tuppence.

LADY IN DISGRACE

A Jove Book / published by arrangement with the author

PRINTING HISTORY
Jove edition / October 1993

ISBN: 0-515-11215-1

A JOVE BOOK®
Jove Books are published by The Berkley Publishing Group, 200 Madison Avenue, New York, New York 10016.
JOVE and the "J" design are trademarks belonging to Jove Publications, Inc.

PRINTED IN THE UNITED STATES OF AMERICA

10 9 8 7 6 5 4 3 2 1

One

Miss Odelia Turnbull tucked a stray gray curl under her cap and lifted her chubby hand to adjust the tube of the telescope as it nosed between the lace curtains. She focused on the chaos on the other side of the copper beeches that separated Marsdon Hall from Musgrove Manor. The manor, a sprawling ivy-covered brick structure in the Elizabethan style with mullioned windows and a multitude of grimy chimney pots, had been built on a slight incline and was surrounded by stately elms. A weedy lawn rolled toward a poplar-lined drive that curved and twisted to the bottom of the park and the imposing iron gate.

The new owner would surely chase the neglect from house and grounds, she mused as she viewed a tiny olive-skinned foreigner wearing a white turban around his head and some caftan-like garment that swept the gravel as he walked toward the house. Surely, that wasn't him. Indian servants, if she guessed correctly. All manner of outlandishly dressed attendants milled around the yard and shifted the untidy piles of luggage. Baskets, boxes, and painted trunks were beyond counting. She wouldn't have been surprised to see an elephant hung with bells amble up the lane with the new owner, Viscount Perth, on its back.

That would be him, she mused as she observed a tall,

broad-shouldered gentleman step out of a black traveling chaise. Such dark hair, and such sun-bronzed skin. That man had been under a foreign sun for a long time, no doubt about that. Thirtyish, she believed, and stylishly dressed in a flawless blue coat, a well-tied neckcloth, and yellow pantaloons.

"Oh my God, he has a monkey on his shoulders!" she exclaimed to her niece. "Such uncouth foreign creatures."

"A monkey? Are you spying on the new neighbor, Aunt Oddy? It's rude," Joanna admonished in a stern voice, but Oddy didn't move an inch.

"Nothing much else to do in this godforsaken corner of Sussex," Oddy said matter-of-factly while watching the progress of an older Indian lady carrying a basket in one hand and a birdcage in the other. Her orange-gold sari shimmered in the sharp sunlight.

"Fiddlesticks! I can think of twenty chores that need doing this morning. Weeding and watering, for instance." Joanna pushed Oddy's silver-gray Persian cat, Penny—or was it the identical Tuppence?—off her sketches on the table. "I'm going to pile compost onto the south corner of the rock garden and plant some creeping phlox today. Purple and white mixed, I think. The flowers should look very pretty in May next year."

"I wish you would pay some attention to your new neighbor, Jo. I heard Viscount Perth is rich as Croesus, and he's a *bachelor*. If you married him, all our problems would be over." Oddy sent a glance of dismay on the damp patch on the wall under the window where the rain had entered during the last storm. "There was some kind of scandal in that family in the past, though, but I can't recall who it involved." She heaved a sigh. "Anyway, when his grandfather dies in Scotland, Perth will become an earl. Such a catch for a lovely woman like you, Jo."

"Hope springs eternal, Aunt Oddy." Laughing hollowly, Joanna rose. "You have naught but rose-colored dreams, and they will not see me to the altar. You know very well that no gentleman in his right mind will marry me."

Oddy gave an unladylike snort. "That's humbug. Lord Thistlethorpe is eager to put a ring on your finger. If you keep resisting him, he'll force you to the altar at sword's point. God knows he has the power to do it, but I wouldn't marry him if he were the last man on earth."

Joanna gave another brittle laugh. "Very bluntly put, but true. I fear Lord Thistlethorpe's plans for me."

Oddy gave her a quick smile. "Take heart. Thistlethorpe is too old to make a serious threat."

Her niece was a darling—sweet-tempered and generous and loyal. Perhaps a trifle too stubborn for her own good, but that was the only flaw Oddy could detect. To match Jo's generous disposition, Nature had given her a strong angular body, an abundance of golden curls that were gathered into a simple bun, and eyes that were bluer than cornflowers. Humor glittered brightly in the blue now, as it often did.

Yes, Jo was a delightful companion, and Oddy hoped they would always share a home—that is, if Lord Thistlethorpe didn't see fit to force them out of this ramshackle place they called home. If only they had some strong gentleman to protect them! It was unfortunate that Jo had scorned all amorous advances since the scandal involving that scoundrel, Leslie Frinton. It was more than unfortunate; it was a disaster. Jo was five-and-twenty, and she ought to have half a dozen toddlers tugging at her apron strings by now.

"I'm not going to set my cap at Viscount Perth, Aunt Oddy. He'll have plenty of young ladies to choose from once it becomes common knowledge that he has returned to England, as wealthy as the Golden Ball. He'll be deluged with invitations from hopeful mamas."

"You could be the first to try your luck, dear." Oddy

returned to her spying and saw the monkey scuttle across the lawn toward the copper beeches. "Oh my, that creature is heading this way!"

"The viscount?" Joanna asked dryly.

"No, you silly. The monkey."

Joanna joined her at the window. "This I must see."

Oddy made space and gave her niece the telescope. "Take a look at the viscount while you're at it. He's standing on the steps talking to a foreign-looking gent in a turban."

Oddy left the room, and Joanna found herself spying between the curtains like a shameless busybody. There were scores of that ilk in Hasselton Village, and Joanna didn't want to turn into one from lack of other amusements.

Penny—or was it Tuppence?—rubbed against her ankles as she studied first the monkey, then the viscount. The gentleman looked imposing even at this distance, and Joanna pictured him ordering his servants about in a stentorian voice. A proud figure of a man, and evidently at ease among the scurrying servants. All the scattered luggage and the colorful minions reminded Joanna of the spectacles at Astley's Amphitheatre in London—clowns, acrobats, and magicians with their tools.

The monkey scuttled in among the trees, a bright red harness dragging behind. No one seemed to have noticed the animal. Joanna put the telescope down and scooped up the cat so that she wouldn't trip over her. "Let's go and greet your new neighbor. You must promise not to scratch out its eyes." Laughing, she held up the cat and glanced at the tiny tuft of white fur on its belly. Tuppence. It was the only visible clue as to the identity of the cat she was carrying. The feline twins had uncannily similar personalities.

"Let's find it, Tuppy." Joanna stepped into the cool, shaded backyard where she had planted every shrub and every bulb that now flowered in shades of red and pink. The scent of lilacs sweetened the air. Spring was at its peak, and Joanna spent every spare minute among her beloved plants.

Due to the scandal that had besmirched her reputation, she didn't have many friends in Hasselton—or elsewhere. As if following the decree of some unspoken law, the gentry shunned her as if she had the plague. She could hear the whispers every time she went into the village—"There goes the hussy who stole a betrothed gentleman from his fiancée." Not that it was true, but no one had believed her innocence—no one but Aunt Oddy.

A stab of bitterness poisoned her mood, and she strove to push away the dark thoughts. Her peers had chosen to believe that she'd tempted Leslie to behave ungentlemanly, and it was a disappointment she had to live with. Even if she hadn't tempted him—it was rather the other way around—she had spent time alone with him, kissing him in a dark room. Such wanton behavior had been enough to ruin her reputation. She blushed at the memory of their heated kisses, and—more. She wouldn't make the same mistake again—fall in love with some self-serving scoundrel. Leslie Frinton had not been a gentleman in the true sense of the word.

The sun shot golden spears among the trees and tossed golden coins on the ground. Joanna walked toward the spot she'd seen the monkey disappear. The cat was wiggling to get down, and Jo set her among the ferns growing beside the path. Tuppence stiffened as the leaves above rattled ominously some distance away.

"I saw the monkey heading this way," cried Aunt Oddy behind her. She was wearing sturdy leather gloves and carried a fish net by its wooden handle. "I'll catch the creature with this. Then we'll return it to its rightful owner and introduce ourselves." Aunt Oddy beamed. "A splendid opportunity we can't let pass."

The leaves rustled and shivered above their heads, and from among the foliage a wrinkled face bordered with a ruff of grayish fur shot forth, staring at them with quick jeweled eyes. The monkey chirped, and a slender gray-brown body swung down, sinewy arms gripping a branch. The long tail slapped Aunt Oddy's face, and she yelped, taking an involuntary step backward—into a patch of nettles.

"Ohhh, the beast *touched* me," she wailed, and brushed her face desperately.

"It's just a playful monkey, not a poisonous snake," Joanna said, but she was hesitant to touch the animal even though it looked friendly enough.

At her feet, Tuppence hissed ominously. With her fur on end, the cat had doubled in size. The monkey chattered at her, and Tuppence started growling, backing in under Joanna's skirt. Joanna could imagine the scratches that might groove her legs if Tuppence was startled into action. She stood very still, watching the monkey swinging from one arm and beckoning with the other—at least, the gesture looked like beckoning. It made a noise like a laugh, then jumped from the branch straight into Joanna's arms.

Jo inhaled sharply, stiff with discomfort at first. But when Tuppence (and her claws) fled back to the house, her ears flat and belly low to the ground, Jo relaxed. The monkey threw its arms around her neck and kissed her on the cheek with leathery lips. She hugged the warm, muscular little body and laughed in delight.

Aunt Oddy babbled beside her, weaving away from the nettles as if drunk.

A young man appeared on the path. "Siddons! Siddooons! Where are you, you plaguey old varmint? There's . . . the little nuisance," he said hesitantly and, blushing, stared at Joanna. "She always darts off before I have time to turn around."

"Now listen here, mister, my niece is not a nuisance," began Aunt Oddy, then swallowed her words as she evidently thought this was the viscount. Too young in Joanna's opinion. Aunt Oddy's mouth looked remarkably like a belly button, and her eyes were round as saucers ringed with spiky pale eyelashes as she viewed the stranger.

"You're . . . you're Viscount Perth," she began.

The young man shook his head and laughed as the monkey jumped into his arms. "No, but I know I look a bit like Uncle Terence." He bowed as far as the clinging monkey would let him. "I'm Toby Brownstoke, from the other side of the village. I just came down from Oxford, and a happy time it is, what with my studies finished and my uncle back from heathen parts." He shifted his weight from one foot to the other, then back again. His flush deepened. "I—I'm frightfully sorry—"

"Brownstoke? Well, I know . . . used to know your mother once," said Aunt Oddy in a tight voice.

Toby's brown eyes widened in recognition. A cowlick fell over his smooth brow, making him look lost and defenseless. "Miss Turnbull, isn't it?" He gave Joanna a guarded glance. "Then you must be Miss W-Warwick."

Joanna smiled ruefully. "The infamous Miss Warwick, no less. I'm sure you've heard everything about my sins from the villagers."

He shrugged. "Yes . . . but I don't care much for gossip. No . . . I like to form my own opinion."

Not completely helpless, Joanna thought, liking the young man. He looked around, seeing the teapot still on the table under a wide canopied maple tree where Joanna and Oddy had breakfasted earlier. "I don't suppose you would have a spot of China tea? The stuff my uncle serves is only fit for pigs. He's a staunch supporter of India tea, y'see, and he's made Mother into a convert. I haven't had decent tea in days."

Joanna glanced at Aunt Oddy, who nodded vigorously.

"Of course we have a cup of China tea." She returned to the garden, followed by Toby and Aunt Oddy, who scratched her ankles surreptitiously.

"In return, perhaps you can tell us all about your uncle," Aunt Oddy suggested shamelessly as she cleared the table and went inside to ask their only servant, Mrs. Dibble, the cook, to put on the kettle.

"That'll be a Canterbury story," said Toby with a sigh, "for when the tea has wet my whistle."

The monkey snatched half a muffin from a plate and hid it behind its back.

"A sneaky one," Joanna said, laughing. "What's her name?"

"Uncle Terence named her Siddons, after the actress." He addressed the monkey. "You're always play-acting, aren't you Siddons?"

The monkey pulled her long lips into a pucker and smacked Toby loudly on the cheek.

Toby chortled and Joanna joined in. She realized this was a special morning. She sensed sudden change in the air, as if some positive force was beginning to blow through her life. It had started with the new owner of Musgrove Manor taking up residence, and now this young man dared to speak to her as if she wasn't the pariah of the village.

Aunt Oddy returned with a tray. She arranged the china on the white tablecloth and placed a plate of still-warm muffins out of reach of the greedy monkey paw. Siddons draped herself around Toby's neck and stared at Joanna with unblinking wise eyes. Beguiled, Joanna exclaimed, "Such an endearing creature! I've never seen a monkey at such close range before. Not even at the Exchange in London."

"Do you want two spoons of sugar, young man?" Aunt Oddy asked militantly.

"Yes, please, and milk." He scratched his ear in embarrassment. "I'm not so *young,* Miss Turnbull. You sound just like my grandmother, who can't accept that I'm almost one-and-twenty. On the fifth of July, I'll be my own man, and Uncle's guardianship will be over." He stirred his tea. "Mind you, Uncle Terence isn't bad for a guardian, but he knows how to make you keep your place without as much as a hard word. I wouldn't want to go against his wishes."

"He sounds formidable," Joanna said, and offered him a muffin and a dish of strawberry preserve.

"He is. One stern look from him, and one's toes start to wither in one's shoes."

Within ten minutes, he'd eaten five muffins, giving loud praise to Mrs. Dibble's cooking. His appetite was appeased, and so was his shyness. He showed no inclination to leave.

Siddons had jumped up into the maple tree, and she was swinging her tail dangerously close to Oddy's face. Joanna thought for a second that her aunt would give it a hard tug. Siddons would be sorry if she got on Aunt Oddy's wrong side.

"Your uncle spent some time in India, didn't he?" Oddy asked curiously. "Not that I want to pry, mind you."

Toby nodded, eying the muffin plate. "He had his own shipping company in Calcutta. Invested heavily in silks and spices. He maintains India tea will be all the rage in the future."

Aunt Oddy sipped her China tea with a proprietary air. "Oh, I'm not sure about that!"

"Have you been to India?" asked Joanna, trying to steer the conversation away from the viscount. She was appalled at Aunt Oddy's intrusive questions, but Toby didn't seem to mind.

"Yes, I visited Uncle Terence for a year. It was dashed hot out there; I could have melted on the spot.

Uncle had a nice house in Calcutta, and a country retreat in the jungle." He shivered visibly. "Retreat sounds too tame. They hunted man-eating tigers there, and I don't hold with that sort of thing. Don't like to kill—"

"Why did he come back?" Aunt Oddy forged on.

Toby shrugged. "I don't know. Perhaps he tired of the humid heat, or the foreign food. All those spicy curries—dreadful, y'know. He sold his part of the company to his partner and came back. Is here to stay for good, I'll lay. Had a bout of homesickness, perhaps."

Siddons jumped into Joanna's lap and snaked one long arm across the table. Toby snatched the muffin plate away just in time, moving it closer to himself. *One muffin for one piece of gossip*, Joanna thought with a silent laugh. Perhaps it was a low price to pay. . . .

Sucking on the tip of her tail, Siddons cuddled close, and Joanna found that she liked the affection. Siddons seemed more biddable than the cats.

Toby smiled as he watched the monkey. "Uncle Terence only needs to buy a gaudily painted hurdy-gurdy and a uniform for Siddons to be in the entertaining trade. I hear he could earn a pound a day turning the handle at some street corner."

"Surely, he doesn't have to resort to that," Aunt Oddy said, outraged. "I heard in the village that he's a very wealthy man."

"Aunt Oddy!" Joanna thought they'd heard enough for one day. It was too brazen to milk the innocent Toby Brownstoke for information. Even though Aunt Oddy was a dear, she was an inveterate gossip.

"Uncle Terence is no pauper." With practiced skill, Toby swallowed the last muffin almost whole, then patted his lips with the linen napkin. "I should go back lest they think I fell into a fox hole." He rose and bowed to Joanna, his eyes warming more each time he looked at her.

"May I come again, Miss Warwick?"

"Yes . . . of course. Your uncle might forbid you to see me, though, once he discovers that his neighbor is a lady in disgrace."

"Oh no, Uncle Terence is a fair-minded man. I know what they say about you in the village, Miss Warwick, but I assure you, Uncle Terence doesn't listen to gossip. He's stern, but he's honest. He doesn't judge people without knowing them. You'll like him immensely, Miss Warwick, and I know he'll like you."

Toby might have changed his tune if he'd overheard the conversation Lord Perth had with Mrs. Brownstoke in her boudoir two weeks later. The overcast day sent gloom into Drusilla Brownstoke's house on the south side of Hasselton, and her sounds of distress—distinct snuffles—from behind her lace-edged handkerchief added to the woeful mood.

"I'm telling you, Terence, that *hussy* has got her clutches into Toby. He spends every waking minute at her house, that dreadful Marsdon Hall with its snarl of shrubs and trees. He speaks of nothing else, and I'm frightened for the future—his future."

"Surely you're exaggerating, Dru. Toby might be a moonling, but he's not addle-brained." Terence gave a thin smile, and Drusilla viewed it with misgiving. Her unpredictable brother would not lift a finger to help, or would he? A very difficult man to read was Terence. He didn't like nonsense, so she tried to speak clearly and without rambling. Such a strain it was to evaluate every word before one spoke. . . . She viewed the stern face of her younger brother and swallowed the repetition of her plea. *Unsettling* was the word that came to her mind as she viewed his smile, and she gulped in apprehension. She so wished he would extricate her poor lamb from that vile person, Miss Warwick, and her poisonous web.

"I haven't seen her yet," he said noncommittally, "but according to Toby, she's a veritable angel."

"Ahhh, Terence, you shouldn't listen to him," Drusilla wailed, and clutched her painful forehead. "He's infatuated, can't find a flaw in his beloved. But I know the conniving mind behind that angelical façade. Mark my words, she has her heart set on dear Toby's inheritance. In one month, he'll be a wealthy man, and that hussy is ready to step in and spend his money. How will he ever prevail against her wiles? He plans to *marry* her, Terence. He told me so this morning. What in the world am I supposed to do?" She dabbed at the corner of her eye, too distraught to see an end to this tunnel of darkness into which Toby's *traitorous* actions had thrown her.

"Toby is a grown man—if inexperienced. I suppose I must disentangle him from this woman, if what you say is true. One can't reason with man in the violent throes of calf love."

Drusilla watched her brother with new hope. He was standing at ease by the fireplace, dangling his eyeglass on its velvet ribbon. He always maintained a picture of male elegance, tall and well-dressed in a Weston coat of blue superfine, faultless linen, buckskins, and shining topboots. Comparing his tall, muscular body to her own dumpy lines, she didn't believe they had shared the same father. Not that she would ever voice such a horrid suspicion. . . .

"I can't extol the depth of my gratitude, Terr— Terence." She remembered in the nick of time that he so hated to be called Terry. "How are you going to do it?"

"Like all hussies, I suspect she'll be susceptible to an offer of money. Five hundred pounds, perhaps. That should take care of your problem."

"Five hundred! That's a fortune, Terence. *I* don't have such deep pockets." She stared at him speculatively from behind her handkerchief. It was of utmost importance to make him put up the funds. After all, he had barrels of gold while she merely "scraped by" on ten thousand a year.

"Hmm, I suppose I'll make the offer and see what happens. Perhaps there's another way out."

"What if she won't accept?"

"I might go as high as one thousand if need be. That should take care of it. Not that I'll make Toby aware of my scheme. That would only incense his anger and firm his determination to wed the tart." Terence's dark gaze bored into her, and Drusilla felt stripped of every lie she had ever told. He always had that disconcerting effect on her.

"By the way, Dru, what is Miss Warwick's sin? I haven't heard the whole of it."

"Oh dear, I feel quite faint thinking of that old scandal. The year she came out, 1814, she was the toast of the town." Drusilla took a deep shivering breath. "Miss Warwick might be beautiful, but terribly cunning. She took London by storm and could have wed any gentleman she chose. She, however, set her cap at Leslie Frinton, a gentleman who was already betrothed—to the Duke of Lynford's only daughter, Celestine. Miss Warwick enticed Frinton into her arms and evidently seduced him during a ball at his fiancée's house. What I heard is that Lady Celestine went into a decline and jilted him. Disgraced, Frinton disappeared from the London scene, and I haven't seen him since." Drusilla lifted her chin to a righteous angle. "Miss Warwick was ruined on the spot. Such a wanton woman to let a gentleman have his . . . his *way* with her."

"She's been hiding in Hasselton ever since?"

"Yes. She inherited Marsdon Hall from her mother, who hailed from these parts. I believe Miss Warwick has a passion for gardening. Her hands look rough, and her hair is always falling untidily around her face. Her strange aunt, Odelia Turnbull, keeps her company."

The viscount gave a sarcastic smile. "I didn't think you would get close enough to Miss Warwick to view her hands, Dru."

In a flutter of agitation, Drusilla twisted her handkerchief. "I . . . I can't avoid going into the local shops sometimes, even if *she* happens to be there. I never *speak* to her, though, nor do I converse with Miss Turnbull."

"That would be a mistake," Terence said with wry amusement.

Drusilla stared at him uncertainly. One never knew with Terence. Had she heard a hint of derision in his voice?

"I take it you want me to engage on this mission posthaste," he continued.

"The sooner the better, of course, but you must do as you see fit, Terence. I have every confidence that you will succeed in solving this problem for me. I'll be eternally grateful, of course." Her voice trembled and rose an octave. "You must beware of falling into the hussy's net. As you know, Toby is not the first gentleman to have succumbed to her charms."

"Rest assured, I won't be taken in by the trollop's schemes. I'm not wet behind the ears like Toby." He raised one slim brown finger. "Remember, it's of utmost importance that Toby doesn't hear of this plan."

"My lips are sealed, Terence dear." Drusilla wrung her hands. "I'm so glad that you're back!"

"I'm not sure I am. I had quite forgotten this damp weather and the small-minded English villagers." He strode to the door. "I shall pay Miss Warwick a visit. She'll be sorry she enticed Toby into her boudoir."

Two

Joanna brushed dirt from the old smock she always wore when she was gardening. Not that it made the garment look any cleaner, but she knew Aunt Oddy hated dribbles of dry soil on her gleaming floors. If the rest of the house belonged to Joanna, the floors were definitely Aunt Oddy's, and she kept them sparkling clean. After the charwoman, who came once weekly, had swept and dusted, Aunt Oddy took out her waxes and polishes, secret ingredients that she had mixed herself, and got to work.

If Aunt Oddy kept the house spotless, Joanna kept the garden a haven of colors and heady scents. She added more perennials each year, and all through the season, something was always in bloom. Sometimes she sat by the lavender border and watched the bees for hours. She had five beehives that she emptied of honey herself every summer and autumn. She helped the bees, and the bees helped her in perfect harmony. Why couldn't people live in such harmony with each other?

"Joanna . . . Joaaanna!" Aunt Oddy called from behind the flowering lilac by the back steps, her hand shading her eyes against the glare as the sun broke through the clouds. She sounded agitated. Emerging from behind the rock garden, Joanna could see her aunt's plump form dressed in a brown muslin gown and a crisp apron.

"Yes?" Joanna's hair had fallen in a tangled mass down her back, and she hastily wound it up and pushed it under the battered straw hat with its faded blue ribbons. She walked briskly toward the house, pulling off the gardening gloves as she went. A shiver of unease traveled through her as she sensed that something had happened to disturb the peace at Marsdon Hall.

"You must come in at once," said Aunt Oddy in a theatrical whisper as Joanna reached the kitchen entrance. "We have an important visitor kicking his heels in the parlor."

"A visitor? Toby?" Joanna had gotten used to her new friend—and admirer—visiting every morning and helping her in the garden. Toby was cheerful company and his infatuation lifted her spirit. The poems he composed proved his adoration. Not that she returned those feelings. Toby's calf love amused her, and she knew it was only a matter of time before he would fall in love with someone his own age, or younger. Anyhow, it felt good to have a new friend after so many friendless years.

"No! Not Toby." Aunt Oddy's eyes bulged. "His *uncle*. He's wearing a face like a thundercloud. The fat is in the fire now, I'll wager." She wrung her hands. "Not that I know why he should be angry, but I'm sure the matter involves Toby."

They entered the kitchen, and Aunt Oddy gave her a critical stare. "Joanna dear, you ought to change your clothes and wash your face. You have a streak of mud on your left cheek, and your arms are quite dusty."

Joanna wiped her face with the back of her hand. "I don't care—"

"Think of your reputation, Jo. You must make yourself presentable before you see the viscount. After all, the gentleman is a bachelor. You must endeavor to look your best—"

"Certainly not, Aunt Oddy." That pronouncement killed any possibility of making herself presentable. "The worse I look, the better," Joanna muttered rebelliously as she stalked through the dark corridor to the front hallway. She moved toward the parlor on the right. It had once been called the rose salon, but the sun had faded the rose brocade on sofas and chairs to a streaky gray.

Joanna stepped over the threshold and viewed the broad back of the gentleman standing by the tall window. Every inch of him looked stubborn, she judged, but when he turned around, every coherent thought fled from her mind. His dark gaze robbed her of her breath, and to her chagrin, her heartbeat quickened. He had a face that demanded scrutiny, carved in bold lines with a decidedly pugnacious chin. A dip at the top of his aristocratic nose pulled attention to his straight eyebrows—black horizontal exclamation marks that gave his face distinction. He wasn't handsome in the classical sense, but she suspected he would stand out in any crowd with that commanding air and piercing gaze.

Nothing slipshod about him, Joanna thought as she viewed his faultless attire. His taste ran toward simplicity and quality. He had not the penchant for florid waistcoats—like Toby. This gentleman gave the impression of always being in control of himself and the world around him.

She wished she'd taken Aunt Oddy's advice and changed her clothes.

"Miss Warwick, I presume," he drawled, and viewed her through his quizzing glass and gave a stiff bow. He stepped toward her, barring her way, a maneuver which prevented her from making herself comfortable in one of the chairs. Her spine stiffened with premonition of the verbal blows to come.

"Yes . . . and you're Viscount Perth. I would like to offer you some refreshments, but I take it you haven't come to pay your respects."

He shook his head. "I have not come in the guise of a friendly neighbor." His gaze insolently traveled the length of her body, and Joanna blushed. He would not look like *that* at a *lady*. He gave a back-handed wave as if reducing her to the level of a servant. She tightened her hand into fists as her anger started to simmer. She couldn't abide insolence. She had done nothing to earn it.

"I don't see that we have any connection other than being neighbors, Lord Perth. And if your visit is not neighborly, I must ask you to—"

"Don't speculate on my intention if you don't know why I'm here, Miss Warwick." He placed his hands on his back and rolled on the balls of his feet. His face had hardened to rock, and ice chilled his obsidian eyes.

"I beg you to state your business with us, Lord Perth, then leave," she said in freezing tones.

"Not *us,* Miss Warwick, *you.* I have no quarrel with your aunt."

"I don't recall ever speaking with you before, Lord Perth, let alone quarreling." Joanna swept by him and sat down on the sofa at the opposite side of the room. Every inch of her was stiff with wrath. She fought for control of the situation, but her act to move away from him didn't change his persecution. He simply turned toward her and looked down his nose as if lecturing to a wayward child.

"It's not yet a quarrel, but it might become one." His voice lowered a notch, to a smooth dangerous purr. "From this day, I expect you to stay away from my nephew, Tobias Brownstoke."

Joanna gave a startled laugh. "Stay away from Toby? Surely he's old enough to choose his own friends."

Seething, she glowered at her new neighbor. *What infernal gall, coming here to lecture me!* "I resent—"

"True that he's old enough, but not old enough for you, Miss Warwick," he continued in that deadly purr. "I have Toby's best interests at heart. What will it take to sever your connection with him? A few seed packets, some tree plants? A new beehive, perhaps?"

Joanna's fury quickened to gale force. His utter contempt reopened the miserable wound that the old scandal with Leslie Frinton had given her. Her peaceful life in Hasselton had slowly healed that wound, but the skin of the scar was brittle. She deeply resented any slur on her gardening hobby, her reprieve. "Please leave the way you came, Lord Perth, and don't show your face in this house again."

His lips widened in a cold smile. "I won't leave until I have fulfilled my purpose. You shan't see Toby again."

"Then tell Toby that." With difficulty, Joanna squelched the urge to slap his face.

"That would only increase his ardor, don't you see? No, that's entirely out of the question. How much will it cost me? How much for Toby's freedom?"

Joanna struggled to keep her voice level. "You're out of your mind!"

"Five hundred pounds. I offer you that much." He sent a speaking glance at the peeling plaster and the damp stains on the walls. "It looks like you could use a new roof, and a multitude of other repairs."

"I find it highly offensive that you would come into my home—a veritable stranger—and tell me what I need." Joanna rose and pointed toward the door. "Now leave!"

The viscount's face darkened. "Five hundred is my offer. Too little, is it?"

"Go!" Joanna shouted, rapidly losing control.

"One thousand, then. Not a penny more, not a penny

less." He made a gesture as if tossing a handful of farthings to begging children.

Joanna laughed shrilly, hating every inch of the man in front of her. He represented everything that had ruined her life; he showed his male contempt, his aim to crush her, and Joanna vowed she would not stand for any more insults from the likes of him.

"Listen you . . . you *oaf*, and don't say another word until you understand my reply. *No.* N–O. I will never take your money. Not now, not ever. Now leave before I throw you out, on the spikes of my pitchfork."

He laughed in derision, and Joanna's last hold on her self-control burst. She slapped his face. She had never done that to anyone before, but the action soothed her fury. He had no right coming into her house offering her money as if she were a street woman!

She could clearly see the red finger marks on his lean cheek. At least the abrupt gesture had stopped his laughter.

"You are a brute, Lord Perth, and I detest you. Now please leave, or I shall report you to the local lawmen for trespassing."

He didn't say another word, only scooped up his hat and strode to the door. Joanna had a sinking feeling she hadn't seen the last of him.

Terence Farnsworth, Viscount Perth, left Marsdon Hall in a cold fury. No female had ever slapped him before, and he was so angry that he saw a red haze simmer before his eyes. What consummate effrontery. He'd been so sure she would accept his generous offer, but he'd been mistaken. Was she fishing for more? That must be it! He wouldn't give her a penny above one thousand. If that. No, he would find a way to extricate Toby from her without spending a single farthing. Not one copper piece would be wasted on the hussy!

A sinking feeling of defeat went through him as he

untied the reins of his chestnut stallion by the gate. Knowing a rare uncertainty—he'd hadn't had that sensation since he was an adolescent—he swung himself into the saddle. For a moment he'd lost control, and he hated it. He'd lost it to a conniving *wench* with eyes the rich blue color of the sapphires adorning the crowns of Indian maharajas.

As he turned his mount toward home, he understood why Toby had fallen so violently in love. Miss Warwick was a beauty with patrician features, a fine cream complexion, and those startling blue eyes. Even if her dress had been ragged and soiled, her bearing had been ladylike and composed. Not the trollop he'd envisioned. Not at all.

Terence wasn't used to defeat. He'd ruled a shipping company staffed with devious British clerks and cunning Indian natives. No one had ever gotten the better of him. Hard, they called him. Unfeeling. He'd heard all the unpleasant epithets before, but those didn't bother him. His British compatriots had asked why he hadn't waited out the demise of his Scottish grandfather, his inheritance, and the title of earl before he immersed himself in trade. He'd evaded the questions. He had no desire to share his past with others, the humiliating flight of his mother and the quarrels with his grandfather. Besides, he had no wish to make public Grandfather's weaknesses, and the fact that the old man had frittered away the family fortune.

Terence sighed and gripped the reins much too hard. Only by sheer determination had he earned back every lost shilling. Deep in his mind, he knew he was trying to restore the family pride that his grandfather had so easily thrown away, but his amassed wealth didn't fill the hollow feeling in his chest.

He hadn't seen the old man for ten years, and he had no plans to ever see him again. Grandfather only reminded him of something good that had rotted. Most of all, it brought back the memory of his faithless mother and her lover. She had been a schemer just like Miss Warwick.

Father had been too weak, Terence thought, ultimately letting her betrayal crush him. *Not me*, he vowed with a flash of fury so hot he wanted to smash something. *No female will ever crush me.*

In the haze of his wrath, he recalled his two courtship failures in India, but he resolutely pushed aside the memories. Dammit, he was sick of ladies who only wanted his money and a lofty title. He had no desire to become the Earl of McBorran when his grandfather died. There was no pride in inheriting that title, not when the current earl was a cruel man without principle.

"Damn you, Miss Warwick," he muttered as the horse cantered through the gate of Musgrove Manor and up the drive. "You'll be sorry you dared to fling my offer in my face."

He left the horse at the stables and went into the house through the south entrance that led past the bailiff's office and a series of guest rooms. He entered his study and slammed the door.

To his surprise, the vast room was not empty. Toby Brownstoke was sitting in the chair by the Louis XV desk reading a book.

"Ah, Uncle Terence, there you are," he said, and looked up with a bemused smile on his face. "Listen to this:

> "See how she leans her cheek upon her hand!
> O that I were a glove upon that hand,
> That I might touch that cheek."

He heaved a deep sigh. "From *Romeo and Juliet.* Dang me, but Shakespeare had a way with words, didn't he, uncle? A decidedly romantic fellow."

"A plaguey old fool. If I hear any more of that farradiddle from you, young whelp, I shall forbid you to visit here again," Terence said darkly.

Toby's eyes widened. "Why look so Friday-faced? A bit of nonsense like this once in a while would cheer you up."

Terence sat down in an armchair and put his feet up on a red and gold-tooled leather hassock that the servants had brought from India. "I went out—"

"Oh! You went to see *her*, didn't you? Premwar told me. She is the loveliest creature alive, don't you think?"

Terence wished his butler had kept his mouth shut. "Hmmm."

Toby's face was all aglow. "Well? What did you think of my intended, my goddess? You must admit she's a veritable Venus."

"That she is, but she has no style whatever. She met me dressed in a brown homespun skirt covered with patches of mud and a straw hat that had a big hole in the brim. I didn't realize she takes so little interest in the social graces." He made his voice neutral so that Toby would not notice the venom he felt inside.

"She's well-mannered enough, and most of the time she dresses prettily, even if her style is sadly out of date. Never a harsh word on her tongue. No, there's breeding there. Joanna's father might have been a wastrel and a gentleman of obscure lineage, but her mother was the daughter of an earl. Her grandfather was the Duke of Stanton."

"She certainly has her charms," Terence said, averting his gaze. *And a strong hand.* "As a barque of frailty—"

"Barque? No, Uncle, much more than that. I know Mother will like her once they meet. Mother was very upset when I announced my intentions to marry Joanna, but she'll come around. She'll find that Joanna is both sweet-tempered and kind. She behaves just as a lady ought to in every circumstance."

Terence remembered the violent slap and smiled grimly. "She certainly has a way with her. I only beg you not to make a hasty decision, Toby. After all, Miss Warwick is an outcast of polite society, and so you'll be if you wed her."

"Pish! That old scandal will be forgotten in time. I shall take her about London. The *ton* will have forgotten *that* little indiscretion."

"I'm not so sure about that. The tattlers' memory is as long as that of an Indian elephant—*very* long, that is." Terence rubbed his fingertips thoughtfully on his left cheek where the skin still tingled faintly.

"Uncle Terence, your support in this matter is important to me," said Toby, rising. He shifted his weight from one foot to the other, then back. "But if I can't have it, you must remember it's only a matter of weeks to my birthday. Then I shall do as I please." He paused, looking uncertain. "But your advice is still welcome."

"Perhaps I shall come with you next time you visit Miss Warwick. I wouldn't mind knowing her a bit better." *And discover her weak points, before I launch my next attack.*

Toby's face lit up. "Of course you must come. Miss Warwick will be delighted to further your acquaintance. She's much too lonely as it is, what with only her aunt and two cats for company."

"We'll see." Terence thought he might offer her more money, even though he'd sworn to not waste another farthing. What else could he do? Toby was too deeply enmeshed to take any chances. The amorous interlude with Miss Warwick would have to end soon. "Have you already asked her to marry you, Toby?"

"No, but I will promptly. I'm waiting for the right moment. It has to be—"

"What if she says no?"

Toby laughed ruefully. "I think she has a tender spot for me. In time, she'll see the advantages of taking my name."

"I don't want you to be disappointed, Toby."

"I won't be," said Toby with a small frown of consternation. "Why—?"

"I hope not." *She'll be delighted when I offer her five thousand pounds. Then you'll be out on your ear, Toby, so fast you won't have time to say "poppycock."*

Three

Joanna thought as she got up the next morning that the day would be entertaining—despite the fact that she still fumed from yesterday's encounter with Lord Perth. If ever he had the gall to enter Marsdon Hall again, she would report him for trespassing!

She wished that her meeting with their new neighbor had been amicable. She had no desire to fight with anyone, let alone with her closest neighbor. But he'd been rude and inconsiderate, never asking her about her feelings concerning Toby, not *deigning* to hear her side of the story. He took for granted that what was said in the village about her was true, and he had treated her accordingly.

She forced her mind shut against the pain that came with the old memories of Leslie Frinton. Sometimes they went around and around in her head while she tried to discover a way to change the past, change the fact that she'd been so starry-eyed as to let Leslie use her. That endeavor was naught but a waste of time. *Don't think about it!* she admonished herself.

She forced herself to go through the plans for the day and pulled off her nightgown. It was Sunday, and after church, she would enjoy her picnic by the lake with Toby and Aunt Oddy.

Her mood had improved by the time Toby stepped

along the brick garden path to find her in the early afternoon. She rose from the flower border and put the trowel and other gardening implements in a bucket. Bees droned around her. The air seemed golden and sweetly scented by flowers.

Toby greeted her with an adoring smile. "Joanna, my dear, today is a happy day when I can rest my eyes upon your lovely face."

Joanna laughed with pleasure. "You're a rogue, Toby, but a kind one."

"I couldn't take my eyes off the clock this morning. The hands moved at snail's pace. I counted the seconds until we could meet." Toby bent over her hand and kissed the fingertips. "Are you ready?"

"Yes . . ." Joanna glanced toward the house and saw Aunt Oddy emerging with a picnic basket and a parasol. Joanna lifted her own parasol from the grass where she'd put it while digging up tufts of dandelion weed. When she straightened, she noticed that a man had followed Aunt Oddy outside. In a second, she had recognized Lord Thistlethorpe, an aging roué whom Joanna would have rejected out of hand except for the fact that he held the mortgage to her home. Any day he chose, he could demand that she and Aunt Oddy move out of the old mansion.

Joanna frowned. The day, which had looked brighter every moment, darkened as misgivings filled her. Lord Thistlethorpe said there was only one way they could keep their house. Joanna had to give him her hand in marriage. The old libertine longed for a young wife; he'd even said as much. His lecherous gaze never left Joanna's body, and she felt defiled in his presence.

Lord Silas Thistlethorpe was a short thin man with an ale paunch sagging the front of his gold-buttoned coat. He admired lurid waistcoats and an abundance of jewelry. He wore a ring on every finger, and his gray hair was curled and pomaded into a stiff formation that reminded Joanna of a galleon in full sail. But his most offensive traits were his clammy hands and a breath that could wilt any plant that came too close to the blast.

Joanna shivered with disgust. She had to be pleasant to him, try to form a plan where she could reject his advances and still keep Marsdon Hall. When no bank, no old friend would help her, she had gone to him for a loan that would clear up Papa's debts. Then Lord Thistlethorpe, who, God knows, had won large sums of money from her hapless father in the past to help speed up his ruin, had stepped forth and offered his assistance.

He gave her a leer as he joined her on the path. "Good afternoon, fairest one."

She must find a way to repay her loan, or all that she had worked for would be lost.

Aunt Oddy looked flustered. "I thought Lord Thistlethorpe would enjoy a picnic with us at the lake," she said, her eyes telling Joanna that she could not possibly turn the tiresome man away.

"The more the merrier," said Toby, missing the underlying tension. Perhaps he believed that Aunt Oddy had her cap set on the old lecher.

"I was lonely—Sunday afternoon is the worst—" said Lord Thistlethorpe, and glanced speculatively at Toby. "I don't think we've met."

"Toby Brownstoke," introduced Joanna. "A good friend of mine."

"Ahhh." Thistlethorpe pushed a spindly finger into Toby's arm. "You're Drusilla's pup. I thought I'd seen you before in the village."

Toby glared at the old man. "Pup, sir?"

Thistlethorpe cackled. "Did I get your goat, *young* man? Well, I'm dreadfully sorry."

Joanna knew he was nothing of the sort. "Shall we

go down to the lake while the sun is favoring us? You never know when a storm will rise on the horizon."

Toby hefted the picnic basket and the party set off along the path that wound down the slope toward the lake at the bottom of the hill. The acres of Musgrove Manor and Marsdon Hall met in a boggy area full of reeds.

Sunlight glittered on the water, ruffles of breeze creating a cascade of diamonds. Ducks quacked querulously in the reeds, and a family of swans glided in the middle of the small lake.

"They'll eat all our bread if we let them," said Aunt Oddy, staring at the swans. "I feed them every morning. Beautiful creatures, aren't they?"

"Uncle Terence said I could use his dinghy anytime," said Toby. "It's moored by the Musgrove dock." He pointed toward the north end of the lake, and Joanna noticed the boat by the new pavilion-like boathouse. A trip in it was a pleasurable prospect, but would the viscount be willing to lend it if he knew Toby's intentions? Joanna shrugged, pushing away the reminder of Lord Perth. Nothing like a breeze on the water to cool off one's brow.

Toby went to inspect the vessel, and Joanna noticed that some of the viscount's foreign servants sat in contorted positions on the lawn outside the boathouse with their eyes closed. This must be yoga, exercises she'd read about in her books on Indian custom. The thin wail of a flute floated across the water from the manor.

Aunt Oddy and Lord Thistlethorpe spread two blankets on the grass next to an enormous weeping willow. Joanna sat down, as far away from Thistlethorpe as possible.

She accepted a glass of homemade applewine from Aunt Oddy and tried to forget that her tormentor was present, sipping an identical glass of wine. She exchanged a worried glance with Aunt Oddy. Was the old man going to press his suit?

"Joanna . . . ?" he wheedled. "You're distant today. Have I come between you and your young admirer now?"

Joanna smiled stiffly and glanced at Aunt Oddy's paling face. "Have no worry. Toby is naught but a good friend, too young to be a suitor. As you well know, I have precious few friends, and I'm grateful for his companionship."

"I've been a good friend to you, and now I want to be more, Joanna. Much more." Lord Thistlethorpe moved to her side of the blanket and sat down—much too close.

Joanna flinched as his foul breath washed over her.

"You must not forget my offer, dear girl. If you marry me, you'll never have to be poor again."

"And if I don't—?"

He shrugged. "I would be sad to see you lose your home. You must find me selfish and disobliging, but I can't have part of my funds tied up forever in Marsdon Hall, can I?"

"You don't need to be in such a hurry to dispose of Marsdon Hall," Joanna cried bitterly.

"No . . . perhaps not. If only I had a wife to warm my nights, then Marsdon Hall could remain in the family." He stroked her arm, and Joanna jerked away.

She remembered what Aunt Oddy had told her right after Thistlethorpe had given them the loan. Aunt Oddy had been against the transaction, claiming that Joanna didn't want to be beholden to a rake like Lord Thistlethorpe. "Why, his two previous wives died under mysterious circumstances. I'll lay he caused their deaths. Do you want to be the third?"

Joanna remembered those words and shivered. Aunt Oddy was right. She should have found another way to dispose of Papa's debts, except there had been no other way. She gave Lord Thistlethorpe's dissipated face a cautious glance. She associated him with darkness, a dank cellar that held all sorts of secrets—all unpleasant.

"You must give me an answer, Joanna. Since you're showing such a reluctance to make up your mind, let me help you. By this date next month, you must have made a decision. You have four weeks to consider if you want to become my wife and keep Marsdon Hall, or be without a home."

Joanna stood abruptly. She had to get away from her tormentor. "Very well, you shall have your answer then," she said, and hurried toward Toby on the path.

Tears filming her eyes, she noticed that Toby was not alone. The viscount—his face darkened in a frown—was close behind him, Siddons perched on his shoulder.

"I told Terence about our picnic, and he insisted that we make up a party. I couldn't refuse him since the lake is part of Musgrove Manor."

"Of course. We wouldn't want to trespass," Joanna murmured, and glared at the viscount over Toby's head. She hadn't known the lake was part of Musgrove land, or she would not have come. It hadn't used to be, but the viscount must have bought it when he purchased the estate.

Siddons chattered a greeting and jumped into her arms. Joanna held the monkey close as if seeking protection from the viscount's hostility.

"I suppose Terence will keep Miss Turnbull company," Toby said. "They are about the same age."

"Toby," drawled the viscount, "do I hear a tinge of derision? I'm not yet in my dotage, you know, nor is Miss Turnbull." Siddons jumped back onto his shoulder and pulled at his ear playfully.

"Well, you certainly aren't a greenhorn."

Joanna couldn't help but laugh, delighted to see the tightening of Lord Perth's lips. Toby's insult had been said without the bite of mockery, but the viscount's pride must have received a blow.

"I take it Miss Turnbull will be hard put to choose between Uncle Terence and Lord Thistlethorpe," Toby said. "Though I must admit that I can't abide that old popinjay."

Joanna brushed off her cornflower-blue muslin gown and adjusted her best straw hat, which Siddons had pushed askew. Today, at least, she had dressed as befitted a lady, and she felt more like a peer of the viscount. If he started an argument, she would meet him on equal ground. Anyway, she didn't want to ruin the day for Toby. He hadn't done anything to deserve a quarrel with his uncle.

"How is your planting progressing, Miss Warwick?" Lord Perth asked with stilted courtesy and scratched Siddons' chin. His dark eyes were filled with dislike, and Joanna's stomach clenched with uneasiness.

"I'm planting asters for a colorful autumn. Are you interested in gardening, Lord Perth?"

He gave her a disbelieving stare. "Not in the slightest."

"Beneath your dignity is it?" she asked sotto voce as Toby ambled off toward the food that Aunt Oddy had spread out on the blankets. "A pity. You're missing much simple pleasure. The earth gives back tenfold what you put into it."

The viscount rubbed his chin thoughtfully, and only Joanna noticed the glint of anger in his eyes. "You don't know the meaning of the word dignity, Miss Warwick."

"And I suppose you do? A veritable expert, I take it?"

"Don't mock me, Miss Warwick."

"I suppose you came here to ask us to get off your land, but as long as we're not in the *water*, you can't force us. However much you must hate the idea of me still owning a piece of the shore, I do own it."

His lips tightened further, and Joanna saw the mercurial flash of anger in his eyes. He had particularly fine eyes, dark and sparkling. If he hadn't been so overbearing, she would have found him highly attractive. But she couldn't abide proud, narrow-minded gentlemen who thought highly of themselves and viewed the rest of the world with contempt. The wind ruffled his dark wavy hair, and she stifled a sudden urge to touch it.

"No need to fly into the boughs, Miss Warwick. I meant what I said to Toby: a picnic is an excellent idea on a hot day like today. I suggest we make a truce for the time being."

"So that you can keep an eye on me—and Toby." He offered his arm, and she reluctantly placed her fingertips on the steely muscles of his forearm. A pleasurable tingle went through her as she sensed the strength of him. She hastily pushed that sensation away as they walked toward the group by the willow.

"You have a suspicious mind, Miss Warwick."

"In your presence, I have every reason to be watchful. I vowed to myself that I would report you for trespassing if you ever came to my house again."

He gave a wry laugh. "Then I must struggle to behave in a civilized manner. I don't want to be hauled away in chains to the local gaol."

Joanna couldn't suppress a laugh. "You have a way of making mockery of everything I say, Lord Perth."

"But *you* mock me with your flirtation with Toby."

"Only if you let yourself be mocked." Deeply shaken by his proximity, Joanna pulled away. "You can't begrudge your nephew some romance."

"Only when his beloved is a lady of ill repute and a schemer, to boot." As they neared the others, he stopped and growled in her ear, "Mark my words, you shan't have a penny of his inheritance."

She gave him what she hoped was a withering stare. "Surely you can't chain Toby to a fence post. He must do as he pleases—especially after his twenty-first birthday. We'll be wed then."

He flinched, and she saw that he had a scathing reply on his tongue. If Aunt Oddy hadn't come between them, she would have expanded on her new role of fortune huntress.

"Lord Perth! What a pleasant surprise. Would you like a glass of applewine?"

"Thank you, yes," said Lord Perth with yet another blistering stare at Joanna before sitting down on one of the blankets. The glance had been fashioned to put the fear of God into her, but she didn't scare that easily. She could show him a few dangerous glares herself!

"I daresay we haven't met," said Lord Thistlethorpe, and introduced himself. His shrewd eyes traveled from Joanna to the viscount, and Joanna knew that he wondered under what pretext the younger man had entered the party.

Siddons jumped from the viscount's shoulder to Lord Thistlethorpe's lap, from where she climbed up to perch next to the baron's precarious hair arrangement. She pulled back her lips, baring her teeth, and yanked an oily strand straight out, then dropped it in front of Lord Thistlethorpe's eyes.

"Get the blasted creature away from me," he barked, swatting at the monkey and trying to rearrange his hair.

Siddons's chatter sounded uncannily like human laughter as she jumped up into the willow's swinging boughs.

Joanna chuckled and sat next to Toby, who was heaping a plate full of cold cuts. He smothered a slab of ham with mustard and put it on a slice of bread. "Food tastes so much better outdoors, don't you know?"

Joanna nodded, noticing his youthful appetite with pleasure. Toby had a contagious vigor that made Joanna forget her isolation for hours at a time. He inspired urges to dance, to attend parties, to mingle with people, make friends. None of that was possible, of course, and she felt a mounting dissatisfaction with her reclusive lifestyle.

"What's that sweet smell?" wondered Lord Thistlethorpe, sniffing the air.

"Lilacs," said Joanna, and accepted a slice of spice cake from Aunt Oddy who was laughing at Siddons's antics above.

"From Joanna's garden. I haven't seen any garden so prosperous, nor a gardener so lovely," Toby said with an adoring smile at her.

"Nor one as stubborn," muttered the viscount for Joanna's ears only.

Joanna wondered how he would look with spice cake all over his face.

"Have some cake, my lord," urged Aunt Oddy, and offered a generous offering on a plate. "Joanna made it this morning."

"Certainly. If Miss Warwick made it, I must sample it." He leaned closer to Joanna and whispered, "Is it poisoned?"

"I wish it were," she said primly, and, disconcerted by his mocking gaze, gulped some wine too rapidly. A coughing attack ensued, and the viscount obliged with a series of hearty thumps to her back.

"St-o-o-p, please," she admonished, angry with him for taking pleasure in her discomfort. "You're a monster," she croaked behind her handkerchief.

"And you're a consummate actress. Poor Toby, who hasn't understood your game."

"How do you like your new home, Lord Perth?" interrupted Aunt Oddy.

"I'm settling in. My sister, Drusilla Brownstoke, insists that I sponsor a housewarming ball for the local gentry. She's invited a host of young people in hope that Toby might lose his heart to some young debutante." He gave Joanna a speaking glance, and she gave him her own flanked with daggers.

"I haven't received an invitation," said Lord Thistlethorpe peevishly.

It was uncouth of Thistlethorpe to mention it, thought Joanna, but she waited eagerly for the viscount's reply.

"Nor have these ladies, I'll wager," continued the baron.

"Dashed paltry thing of my mother not to send out the invitations," Toby said between bites. "I'll see to it that you get one."

"That'll be the day," Joanna murmured. "Mrs. Brownstoke would sell her soul to the devil first."

"What did you say, Miss Warwick?" the viscount demanded to know.

"She won't send us one, Toby," she said, ignoring her adversary on the right. "You should not upset her by asking, but surely Lord Thistlethorpe—"

"Mother has no right to judge you," Toby cried, very agitated. "She must see for herself that you're a lady in all the aspects of the word. I won't have her treat my friends—"

"Well, this is a pretty kettle of fish," said Lord Thistlethorpe. "Only because of my innocent statement."

"I will see to it that—" began the viscount, but Joanna interrupted him.

"I think we should drop the subject altogether."

"Joanna," said Toby between bites of bread, "shall we embark on the water now? I'll fetch the boat." He rose, scooping up a bottle of ale.

"That would be most pleasurable," she said, relieved to get away from the party. What had started as a wonderful day had turned into a disaster.

"I'm afraid my gout will prevent me from getting

into that small vessel," said Lord Thistlethorpe. "It'll sway terribly, I'll wager. I have no head for waves."

Joanna stifled a nervous laugh as she viewed the violent waves of his coiffure.

The viscount stretched out his long, muscular legs, and Joanna could not but admire his virile strength. "I haven't had the time to test the waters," he said.

"I spied some of your male servants doing their ablutions in the lake early in the morning one day—indecently attired," the baron said. "Highly irregular, if you ask me."

"Premwar used to take his ablutions in the Ganges. He's a Hindu and believes that the river is holy. Here he can't have the water of his country, but old habits die hard."

"Your entire staff is Indian, my lord?" asked Aunt Oddy, her eyes wide with curiosity.

"No, my bailiff and the housekeeper are British, and some of the maids, but my secretary and personal servants are Indian. I couldn't leave them behind when they worked so hard for me in Calcutta."

Hmmn, Joanna thought, *he isn't entirely without a heart*.

"You've settled near your sister, which is very commendable. I'm certain she feels greatly relieved to have a strong shoulder to lean on after Mr. Brownstoke died. However, isn't your family seat in the north?"

"Aunt Oddy!" Joanna admonished—to deaf ears.

"I hear you're related to the McBorrans. A very old family that."

"Be that as it may," the viscount said in crisp tones, "I rather like living in the south of England."

A noncommittal answer if there was one. Joanna sensed that he was hiding the truth. She didn't blame him for not wanting to air his family business abroad.

Toby shouted from the boat. "Come Joanna, let's sail the seven seas!"

With a sigh of relief, Joanna got up and brushed any stray breadcrumbs from her dress. She raised her parasol over her head and headed down to the dilapidated dock to which Toby was clinging with a boat hook.

From the corner of her eye, Joanna noticed that Lord Perth had fallen into step beside her.

"I didn't attend the picnic to be insulted by you, or have my family business scrutinized by Miss Turnbull," he said.

"Then why did you come?" Her anger started to boil as she sensed that he had an ulterior motive, one that involved her, and an unpleasant one at that.

He didn't reply at once, but finally said as they stepped out on the wobbly dock, "Perhaps I wanted a chance to study the strategy of my adversary."

"I asked you not to come here again."

"I didn't want to ruin Toby's pleasure. He asked me to join the party."

She gave a dry laugh. "And I'm the Prince of Wales. No, whatever schemes you have in mind for me, Lord Perth, won't work."

"Don't trifle with me, Miss Warwick."

"Come on, Joanna, the boat wants to get away from me," Toby shouted. "Uncle Terence, please help her down."

"I suppose I'll have to lift you into the dinghy," the viscount said dourly.

"Don't you dare touch me!" Joanna swung around so that the long fringe of her parasol swept across his face.

The viscount took a startled step back and staggered onto a rotten plank, which cracked with a groan. Before he had a chance to regain his balance, he toppled over the side of the dock and fell into the mud below.

Lord Thistlethorpe cackled from his lookout point on the blanket, and Aunt Oddy squealed. Joanna concealed her laugh behind her hand as she stepped into the swaying boat.

She viewed Lord Perth's enflamed countenance, and her laughter increased. He was sitting in the mud, which had completely drenched his clothes. A smear lined one cheek, and a brown glob dripped on his chin.

Toby joined in the laughter once he'd seen that his uncle wasn't hurt. "Well, one would think you're well over the oar, Uncle Terence, or is it three sheets to the wind?"

"*You!* I'm not finished with you two. You just wait."

Siddons had arrived to investigate the rumpus on the dock. She jumped onto the viscount's head, chattering.

"I think we're finished with you for the time being," cried Joanna.

The viscount glared at her as he heaved himself out of the mud. His eyes brimmed with wrath, and Joanna knew she had only gained a short reprieve in the war with her neighbor.

Four

Early the next morning, Joanna painted a watercolor by the lakeshore. She wanted to capture the sunlight reflected on water before the sun rose any higher. After a night of uneasy tossing and turning, she wondered if this activity would give her the peace she sought. It hadn't to this moment, but she was determined not to let any thoughts of the odious Lord Perth destroy her equilibrium—as they had last night. She chuckled as she remembered his muddy form, but at the same time the memory made her uneasy. She waited tensely for their next confrontation, not knowing when it would occur. If only she knew, she would be ready for him. If he caught her at an unguarded moment . . . well, there was no telling how she would hold up to his verbal assaults. She sighed and threw an acid glance at Musgrove Manor in the distance, the old mansion appearing benevolent in the gilded light of morning.

A flock of birds rose in a cloud from the lawn, and she saw movement by the Perth dock. It looked like craftsmen were working on the hull of a boat.

She put down her brushes and studied the everchanging water. Her thoughts were not on her work, but on the previous day when she'd been in the middle of the lake with Toby. He was charming and sweet-tempered, but so innocent she felt like an old woman even though only a few years separated them. He'd gone down on one knee among the ropes on the bottom of the boat and clutched her hand to his heart.

"Please say you'll become my wife once I am of age, dearest Joanna." Evidently he'd sensed her hesitation. He'd added, "I ask you to seriously consider my offer." He'd looked at her with his pleading blue eyes. She recalled having thrown a glance toward the shore to see if anyone was watching. To her chagrin, her cheeks had warmed when she discovered that the viscount had remained standing by the dock, his arms crossed over his chest. His demeanor had struck her as menacing, and the last thing she needed was another quarrel with Lord Perth. She'd torn her gaze away, as if his hostile stance was trying to strike her down from afar.

"You're the finest young man I have ever met, Toby, but a union between us would never do. I'm too old for you—"

"Balderdash!" A mutinous look came over his face. "I don't care—I wouldn't care if you were one hundred years old." He'd kissed her hand fervently, and Joanna could only feel gratified at his attention. She'd gently pulled her hand away.

"Say that you'll change your decision at the earliest moment," he'd begged, stubborn to the last.

She'd turned the canopy of her parasol toward the shore to block out the view of the angry viscount. "No . . . Toby, I don't love you."

He'd looked crestfallen, put pinched his lips together in determination. She would cherish his friendship, and when he fell out of love with her, they would still be friends. Sooner or later, he'd find someone his own age to love.

She returned to the present, realizing that it would be so easy to give in to Toby's offer of marriage. If she did, all her financial problems would be over. But no, she didn't love him, and she seriously doubted that he loved her. Love was all-important in a marriage. . . .

The sun touched her bare head, and with a sigh, she put on a wide-brimmed straw hat to protect herself from the strong light. The freshness of the morning was gone, and she wasn't sure she'd captured the essence with her brushes. She glanced critically at the painting and decided to pack her tools in the wooden box where they belonged.

She spread out a blanket under the weeping willow with its drooping branches. She tossed down a pillow and stretched out, resting her tired head. Her eyes ached from the lack of sleep, and she closed them, thinking this was a perfect spot for an hour of rest.

One of the Persians, probably Penny, came and curled up beside her and purred. The purr of contentment transmitted peace to Joanna, and she dozed, pleased to be rid of her worries for an hour. Here at least, she would sleep undisturbed. . . .

Terence saw first the easel and the empty stool behind it, then a pair of worn lady's slippers in the grass, then stocking-covered feet sticking out from under the filmy strands of leaves. A tattered blanket, a gray mound of fur, and the pleasingly rounded form of Miss Joanna Warwick completed the picture of bucolic harmony.

She was muttering something in her sleep, and Terence watched her face, so innocent in repose. Was this the same sharp-tongued schemer he'd met before? This moment she looked unspoiled and sweet. His heart softened.

He'd seen her from the dock and decided to stage another confrontation with her, this time armed with an offer that she simply could not refuse. Now he found his anger slowly seeping away, and he wasn't sure what to do.

Confused, he watched her in silence. Her eyelids flickered, and her lips moved as if conversing with someone invisible. Birds twittered in the leafy crown above, and the furry gray mound suddenly grew a head and stared at him with suspicious green eyes. The cat yawned, displaying a pink tongue, the longest he'd ever seen in a cat.

He sat down on the edge of the blanket, still unsure what to do. He ought to leave and return later, but something held him back. The dreamy figure of Joanna Warwick.

She was dressed in a faded blue muslin gown printed with sprigs of flowers. Her hair had sneaked out of the confinement of pins and curled over her shoulders, giving her an air of infinite charm. He wondered what her silky hair would feel like wound around his hands.

Influenced against his will by the dreamy air of the morning, he reached out to discover the texture of her hair. Just as he was about to touch her, she awakened, her blue eyes opening wide in alarm. At first she had difficulty focusing, but as soon as her gaze touched him, she struggled into a sitting position.

"What infernal . . . what are you doing here?" she demanded in outraged tones. She scrambled away from him, drawing up her knees to her chin. He had a delectable view of her ankles, and when she noticed the direction of his attention, she curled her feet under her. The cat stalked across the blanket and sat in front of him, staring at him as if asking the reason for his intrusion. The plumey tail twitched with annoyance.

"What do you want, Lord Perth?" Miss Warwick continued. "You're trespassing."

He tried to summon his anger, but found that the peaceful spot by the lake—the warm air, waves lapping lazily against the shore—had released his tension until only lassitude remained.

"I know I am." He shot her a quick glance, reading

only anger in her eyes. They blazed with blue fire, and something somersaulted in his chest. He could not have explained the feeling had someone asked him about it. A sweet warmth followed, another inexplicable sensation spreading in his chest and clutching his throat until he was speechless.

"I told you I would call in the law if you bothered me again." She curled her arms around her waist protectively and her lips thinned into a stern line.

He hardened his heart and stood. "I came to speak with you." He waited as an uncomfortable silence stretched between them. Suspicion pinched her features and narrowed her gaze. He stiffened further, pushing away any remnant of softness inside.

"If your aim is to bribe me again, I won't listen to another word, my lord. Your gall is the outside of enough."

He knew he had lost—for the moment.

"Actually, I came to look for something I lost yesterday, a valuable diamond pin," he lied.

She didn't move, only stared at him with those lovely cold eyes. "It is probably lost in the mud by the dock," she said.

He detected a hint of glee in her voice. "It amuses you no end that I fell into the mud, doesn't it, Miss Warwick?" He clasped his hands behind his back and stared down at her, using his most intimidating look that never failed to subdue toadeaters and unruly servants.

"Yes, it was a rather amusing event. I hope you didn't cover Siddons with mud. She might catch a chill."

He felt his cheeks grow hot as she bubbled with sudden mirth. She clapped her hands to her mouth and her eyes danced with mischief.

"Siddons was a lot drier than I when all was said and done," he said. Anger churned in his chest, and as he experienced the swift turn in his emotions, he was bewildered. For some strange reason, she had the power to play on his feelings as if they were the wires of a harp. The realization infuriated him. For the second time in as long as he could remember, he lacked complete control of himself.

"Siddons had the good sense to stay out of the muddy water." She was grinning now, like the village idiot that loitered outside the tavern in Hasselton.

He nodded curtly and added a touch of frost to his voice. "Siddons has great circumspection. Sometimes I think she's more intelligent than *any* female in my immediate vicinity."

"I presume that includes me." She got up with one fluid movement and placed a straw hat adorned with a deplorable pink ribbon on her head. God, she was lovely.

"Miss Warwick, if I were you, I wouldn't display quite so much glee."

"Why? Are you threatening me?" She parted the strands of willow and moved away from the shade of the tree. Heading toward her easel, she threw a glance at him over her shoulder. "Again?"

Hot around the collar, he followed her. He longed to grip her shoulders and shake her. "If I recall rightly, you're not wholly without blame concerning the accident. You, or rather your parasol, pushed me off the dock. I can easily imagine what you would look like sitting in the mud. Like in my case—not a pretty sight."

"I suppose you're twitching to throw me in." She gripped her parasol leaning against the stool by the easel. Holding it like a weapon, she aimed the point at him. "Don't even try."

"Don't think of poking me with that! If you can't see the humor in the possibility of your person flung into the mud, I must say your sense of the ridiculous is sadly lacking."

"Don't goad me, Lord Perth. I don't want to do something I'll regret later, and don't say that *my* humor is lacking, when you have none. As I recall, you did not laugh while sitting in the muck."

He pushed aside her parasol and towered in front of her. Gazing at some spot over her shoulder, he said, "You're at my mercy, you know. I could lift you up into my arms and—"

"I'm melting with terror," she chided. Joanna glanced at her adversary between her eyelashes. For some reason his sudden appearance on her turf did not strike her with fear, only drove her to rile him. Her rest had restored her buoyancy, and she was ready to move in any direction he decided to turn their argument. If he thought his high-handed ways would make her cower in fear, he would be sorely disappointed. She was no pudding heart, and if he hadn't learned that—

"If you were boneless, you could no longer stand up," he said practically. He raised his eyebrows in challenge, and a wicked light shone in the dark depths of his eyes.

"Sheer will-power is holding me upright." She thought he looked singularly handsome dressed in buckskins, a blue coat, and faultless linen. A carelessly tied Belcher handkerchief around his neck gave him a rakish air. His chestnut curls ruffled in the light breeze, reducing much of the menace on his face. His chin jutted aggressively, and Joanna noticed a faint cleft she'd not seen before. She found that she couldn't remain untouched by his presence, her emotions rocking like a boat on a wind-tossed sea, from anger to mirth to uncertainty. She could not still her galloping heart and wished he were stupid and wart-faced, thus easier to ignore.

"I would like to know what my greenhorn of a nephew discussed with you during the boat ride yesterday. If I were you, I would not believe a word that young whipstraw says. He changes his mind as often as the wind changes direction."

A twinge of anger went through her. "I'm sure you'd like to wring a confession out of me, but I will not speak. What Toby disclosed is confidential."

His lips curled into a freezing smile. "By your smirk, I surmise you managed to wangle a declaration of undying love from him."

"I am not smiling, and as I said, Toby's secret is secure with me." She stabbed the tip of her parasol into the ground to prove her point.

"I must warn you, Miss Warwick, that Toby has loved before, and each time he discovered that his feelings were simple infatuation, not love."

"What do *you*, pray tell, know about love? The only feeling you seem capable of is loathing. And your manner is sadly lacking in courtesy."

Red spots of anger flared in his cheeks. "I know calf love when I see it, and Toby is woefully afflicted by that malady. Don't pretend otherwise, or you might have a painful fall from ignorance at a later date."

"What an alarming thought." Joanna wished she could kick him in the leg, but such hoydenish behavior she had left behind when she began to put up her hair. "I think *you* are the person ignorant of true feelings, not Toby. He might be young, but I find him very mature for his age, responsible and sweet-tempered. Evidently he didn't inherit those traits from your side of the family."

A tide of wrath seethed in his eyes. "A union with you would completely destroy the good strains of Toby's character. Your children would be shrews and ramshackle here-and-therians. Gamblers and twits."

She gave him what she hoped was a withering stare. "*You* certainly bear an abundance of such characteristics, and as Toby is closely related to you, any union—"

"Do cease, Miss Warwick. You've heaped my head

with a rare lot of insults, and I must point out that my patience is limited." He bestowed a molten glare on her.

"Humbug! Patience you don't have at all, nor do you possess any modicum of finesse. Insults, threats, and bribes won't change my mind in any way, only strengthen my belief that Toby will make a very suitable husband. In the near future."

He clutched his head with one hand, and something like a growl issued from his throat. After giving her a baleful stare, he strode down to the water's edge and glanced toward the other shore. By the stiffness of his shoulders, she could tell that he was at the point of explosion. Joanna almost regretted her acid words, but he'd goaded her beyond endurance. She took a step toward him, almost calling out his name, when Aunt Oddy puffed down the weedy path from the house, clutching a stack of papers in her hand.

Her cap sat askew on her grizzled hair, and her face held a distraught expression.

"Oh, Joanna, I'm all at sixes and sevens," she wailed. Her chubby legs fought through the tall grass. "We got a new set of dunning letters this morning. If we don't pay the merchants soon they'll see us to debtor's prison." She stopped abruptly as she noticed the viscount on the lakeshore.

Joanna frowned in warning, and Oddy clapped a hand to her mouth. It was too late now, Joanna thought, chagrined. Lord Perth had heard every word, and his smile looked positively triumphant.

"Goodness gracious, I had no idea—" said Aunt Oddy.

"I believe we should discuss our problems in private, Auntie."

"Yes . . . yes, of course." Aunt Oddy hid the fist clutching the bills in the folds of her old gown. She gave Joanna a crestfallen glance.

Joanna, battling a wave of exasperation, smiled and

patted her aunt's arm. "I'll join you in the parlor presently."

"You should not chat with Lord Perth unchaperoned, Jo."

"Oh pooh, my name cannot be blackened further. If someone observes me with our neighbor, it will add more grist to the local gossip mill, but that won't change my position. My reputation is beyond redemption."

Aunt Oddy heaved a deep sigh and glanced uncertainly at the viscount as he stalked toward them. He bowed and gave Oddy a haughty stare. Blushing, Oddy glanced away and dithered. "Jo, really. I'd rather you accompanied me inside this minute. 'Tis not right—"

As the viscount apparently was about to voice his opinion, Aunt Oddy fled up the path, a moan of despair erupting from her mouth. Lord Perth looked pleased with himself. "I see that I haven't lost my ability to daunt some people."

"It is excessively rude of you to glare down your nose. I would be ashamed if I were you."

"Rubbish!" He pulled at the cuffs of his coat, and a devil danced in his eyes. "Miss Warwick, I overheard Miss Turnbull as she voiced her concern. I don't think you have much of a choice. If you don't want to find yourself in debtor's prison, you must accept my generous monetary offer. All I ask in return is Toby's release. I don't know what promises he has committed himself to, but consider them null and void."

Joanna twirled her parasol, wondering if she would have the courage to stab him with it. "I have not agreed to take your money. Nothing has changed. In fact, I'd rather go to debtor's prison than be beholden to you."

He apparently weighed her words, all the while staring at her with disapproval. "You're a singularly disagreeable female, Miss Warwick. And greedy. I think you're holding out for a larger sum."

"I don't care a fig for your opinion, Lord Perth. I think it is about time you leave my property. Our conversation has fatigued me no end."

After an awful silence, he said menacingly, "Five thousand pounds, take it or leave it. I won't give you a penny more. It ought to take care of a few bills."

"No!" Dizzied with rage, Joanna flung her parasol as hard as she could into the woods separating the lakeshore and her beloved garden. She hadn't found the courage to slam it into his face. At least his despicable smile was gone. "No. Never. Not as long as I live."

"Shrew!" he shouted after her as she marched up the path, furiously swinging her arms. Strangely enough, that word hurt more than the entire mass of insults he'd flung at her earlier. She fought a bout of tears and vowed she would never speak with Lord Perth again.

Five

"You turned down his offer?" Oddy wailed. *"Five thousand pounds!* I think I will have a fainting spell, and when I wake up, I will discover that you only played a cruel joke on me." Pressing a hand to her temple, she sank down on Joanna's bed.

Joanna stared grimly at the bills spread over the top of her mahogany escritoire. "I thought we paid the butcher and the ironmonger last month."

"Oh, no, we haven't paid them for months, and they won't deliver any more goods. Says so in the letters that accompanied the bills."

"This is a disgrace. I didn't realize our situation was this serious."

"Joanna, you must speak with Lord Perth and tell him you've changed your mind. Accept his offer. Only after we've paid the bills will we be able to walk through the village with our heads held high."

"I have never bent my head in shame, and I doubt you have either," Joanna said a trifle sharply. "You can't insist that I take Perth's bribe. I'd rather go to prison, and I told him so."

Oddy wailed again, a hideous drawn-out sound. "How can you be so stubborn, Jo? I don't recall any member of this family, including your father, who had such a stubborn streak."

"Tenacity will serve us well, believe me. Very soon, Lord Thistlethorpe will arrive on our doorstep demanding an answer from me."

Aunt Oddy flapped her hands in front of her face. "Dear me, whatever shall we do?"

Joanna threw her swooning aunt an exasperated glance. "Trust me, I won't let Thistlethorpe rule our lives, just as I won't let the merchants bully us. I daresay we can scrape together enough funds to pay these bills, and then we shall practice stricter economies." She thought for a moment. "We aren't exactly in the poorhouse. I have decided to give pianoforte lessons. You know there will be plenty of students among the local gentry."

Oddy shook her head. "You're mistaken. No respectable mamas will let their daughters pass our doorstep—or you theirs—and well you know it."

"Well, then I'll offer my services to the merchants. Their sons and daughters will need music lessons, and I am more accomplished than Reverend Grindle."

"Ohhh, don't mention the vicar. His nose is tilted higher than anyone else's in the village. He's positively loath to let us into the church on Sundays, but he can't very well turn us away."

Fighting a bout of bitterness, Joanna turned toward the window. She glanced past the copper beeches and studied the mellow brick façade of Musgrove Manor. If only she could blame her difficulties on her odious new neighbor, but her problems stemmed from earlier times. She was tired of being treated like a leper in Hasselton, and she wished she didn't have to go there at all. But it could not be avoided. Now and then they needed sewing supplies and other items.

"Aunt Oddy, we shall prevail somehow. I won't give up hope, and neither should you. Our ship is still afloat."

Aunt Oddy clucked her tongue, but she uttered no further recriminations.

Joanna saw two of the viscount's Indian servants step onto the lawn. One was carrying an unusual stringed instrument, and the other a drum of some sort. As the shadows lengthened in the afternoon, they began to play. The stringed instrument wailed sorrowfully in the stillness, and Joanna found the rhythm of the foreign music fascinating. One thing was certain. There was never a dull moment since Lord Perth had moved in with his retinue. The Indians didn't know any English customs, but they didn't seem to suffer unduly from this obstacle. Neither would she from hers, she vowed. Somehow she would find a way around her problems.

"Let's take a drive before the sun goes down," she suggested to her wilting aunt. "It will do us a world of good to get away from our difficulties for a spell. When we get back, Mrs. Dibble will have our tea ready."

The village slumbered in the sun, and Joanna urged their only horse on faster to leave High Street behind. Daisy, the mare, lengthened her old rheumatic bones into a canter. The ancient gig with its creaking wheels, the only carriage they owned, bounced over the holes left by the last rain. Joanna smelled the flowering jasmine on the air and inhaled deeply. Ever since her confrontation with Lord Perth, she'd been unable to think of anything but him—except the mounting bills, of course.

She worked in her garden every day, but not today. He had managed to thoroughly shake her out of her contentment, and she suspected she wouldn't have had the patience to weed after she left him on the lakeshore. Drat the man! She wished Toby was present to cheer her up with his chatter, but she'd seen neither hide nor hair of him since she jilted him in the middle of the lake.

The lane wound through a wooded area, and two squirrels chased each other along a branch hanging over the road.

"Look over there," Aunt Oddy said, pointing with her gloved hand.

Joanna glanced toward the clearing and saw a fine dappled gray stallion grazing with the reins dragging behind. "Looks like there might have been an accident. Can you see any sign of the rider, Aunt Oddy?"

Oddy craned her short neck for a better view of the woods. "Not that I can tell."

"We'd better take a look. There's a path among the trees." Joanna jumped down and bound Daisy's reins to a sapling beside the lane. The mare immediately started grazing the lush grass lining the ditch. "Come, let's find out what happened. Mayhap the rider is hurt."

"He, or she, might be miles away."

Nevertheless, Joanna led the way in among the leafy beeches and elms. Birds sang and fluttered in the trees, and a curious finch jumped from branch to branch, following their progress with onyx eyes. Joanna crossed a rickety wooden bridge, Aunt Oddy close behind her, panting from the exertion.

Ahead loomed a crumbling stone wall, round stones piled on top of each other without mortar. Joanna heard a moan and ran forward.

Right below the wall lay a young woman, her eyelids closed in a swoon. A riding crop and hat adorned with gray plume had been flung some distance away.

"The horse must have thrown her," Oddy said, and got down on her knees beside the young lady.

Joanna chafed the thin pale hands of the stranger between her own and studied the fine-boned, sprightly face with its pert nose, pointed chin, and strawberry-red lips. Wispy blond curls framed the countenance, and the small, thin body was clad in an outmoded riding habit of burgundy velvet adorned with black braiding.

The blue-veined eyelids flickered as Oddy pulled the blond head onto her lap. "She looks familiar, but the name eludes me."

"Where am I?" the stranger asked in a small voice.

"Your horse must have thrown you as he jumped the wall," Joanna said.

She gave a moan. "That horrid, headstrong nag. I declare I will hobble him until he's too old to walk." She struggled to sit up and rubbed her eyes.

"Are you in pain?" Oddy asked.

The young lady shook her head. "My breath was knocked out of me, that's all. 'Tis not the first time I've taken a tumble."

Joanna nodded. "I admire your fortitude. By the way, I'm Miss Joanna Warwick, and this is Miss Odelia Turnbull."

The young lady's cerulean eyes widened in recognition. "Oh my, I'm not supposed to talk with you, am I? But who's to know? I'm Annabelle Rushton. Mother and I spend the summers in Hasselton, in my grandfather's old lodge. I'm pleased to meet you."

"Likewise." Joanna nodded, having heard about the Rushtons before. Mrs. Rushton was a captain's widow, and Joanna suspected that they lived a rather modest life on the pension left by Captain Rushton. He'd died at one battle or other during the Peninsular campaign. "If your mama discovers that you've spoken to us, she'll give you a severe rake-down. And she'll be upset when she discovers that your horse threw you."

The young lady shrugged. "Mama can be very tedious at times, but she won't discover what happened here—unless I tell her, which I won't." Annabelle rose and brushed off her riding habit. She wobbled slightly as she stepped onto the path. "I'm so happy to see new faces. I have been bored to flinders in the company of dowagers and old widowers. Mama has the starchiest of friends."

"You have no friends your own age, Miss Rushton?" Aunt Oddy asked as she steadied the younger woman and brushed stray twigs off the riding habit.

Annabelle shook her head. "Please call me Annabelle.

Miss Rushton is too tedious to bear. Where's Jasper? I knew he'd decided to have one of his reckless turns as soon as we approached the wall. I tried to stop him, but he jumped anyway."

"Fortunately you didn't come to any harm." Joanna tucked Annabelle's arm under her own and moved slowly down the path. "You should perhaps ride a more docile mount."

Annabelle shook her head. "I've handled more difficult horses than Jasper. I'm used to his quirks."

"Are you sure you don't need to rest further?"

"Quite certain. I might be an accomplished horsewoman, but that's the extent of my talents." She made a face. "I can't sew a straight seam, and I hate painting watercolors."

Joanna laughed. She already liked the frank Miss Rushton. Like Annabelle, she enjoyed making a new acquaintance. They entered the clearing where Jasper was grazing without a care in the world.

"There he is!" Annabelle extricated herself from steadying arms and stalked up to the horse, brandishing her crop. To Joanna's relief, she didn't strike the stallion, only berated him in a stern voice.

"You rotten, odious brute! I declare I shall send you to the glue factory on the morrow. I know you threw me on purpose." She tugged his black forelock, forcing the large head up.

Jasper cocked his ears and, chewing, gave his mistress an uncaring glance. He whickered in greeting, but that was all the response her threat solicited. He shook off her hand and went to work on a clump of grass at her feet.

An impish smile brightened Annabelle's face. "He is exasperating, isn't he? The brute never listens to me."

"Perhaps you treat him too kindly," Oddy suggested.

Annabelle smiled and scratched Jasper's gleaming gray hide. "I reared him myself. I've known him since he was a newborn foal. If it weren't for that stubborn streak, he would be perfect." She shrugged as if nothing mattered. "I adore him anyway."

Jasper shook his thick mane and whinnied as if he'd understood every word. He pawed the ground with one of his hooves and pranced in a circle.

"Don't pay any heed to him. He's vying for your attention. He wishes he could play a part in the spectacles at Astley's in London."

"He's a handsome horse," Joanna said.

"Mama says it costs too much to feed him."

Aunt Oddy chuckled. "He's happy as a grig grazing Lord Perth's grass."

Annabelle laughed, a high merry sound. "I wonder what Perth would make of Jasper chomping away at his grass? The viscount is a stern gentleman, but he gave me permission to ride on his land. Mama thinks he's interested in me and tries to throw us together at every turn." She sighed. "I'm mortified at Mama's behavior. Lord Perth is the last person I would wed, even though I have pitifully few suitors."

"I'm surprised," Aunt Oddy said. "You're a lovely young lady, and I believe a lot of gentlemen would be happy to offer for you."

"I'm sure you know already that the Rushtons don't have a feather to fly with. No one wants to marry a penniless gentlewoman."

The words echoed in Joanna's head. She had spoken the exact words many times to Oddy.

Annabelle gathered Jasper's reins and walked him onto the road. "I'd better return home before Mama sends out a search party." She turned to them and beamed a smile. "Thank you for your help."

"Never mind. I wish I could invite you to tea, but your mother would not allow you into our house," Joanna said, feeling sad that she should lose a new friend so quickly.

Annabelle tossed her head. "Mama doesn't know everything I do."

"I'm surprised she allowed you to ride out alone," Aunt Oddy said.

Annabelle giggled with youthful vigor. "She didn't, but I got rid of the groom outside the village. None of the horses in our stables can keep up with Jasper." She pointed toward the gig. "May I use your carriage as a mounting block?"

"Of course." Joanna released Daisy's reins and watched as the younger woman lifted herself agilely into the side saddle.

"It wouldn't do to return home leading Jasper by the reins. I would have to answer too many questions." Annabelle waved, and Jasper galloped down the lane toward the village.

"Quite a spirited young lady," Aunt Oddy said. "I'll wager she gives her mother nervous turns frequently."

Joanna laughed and helped her aunt into the gig. "A refreshing young woman. At that age, most ladies have nothing to say for themselves."

"Except discussing the latest *on-dits* and fallals of fashion—not that I'm not partial to both myself." Aunt Oddy cleared her throat. "I'll own gossip is one of my weaknesses."

"And what would the other weaknesses be?" Joanna asked, and winked.

Oddy bristled. "If you think you can force me to divulge—"

"Don't fly into a pet, dear Auntie. I know you like your tea with a tipple of brandy at night. There's nothing to be ashamed of." Joanna inhaled deeply. "I wish I could furnish you with a new gown and a box of candied fruit, but to keep Marsdon Hall we must wear rags on our backs."

Oddy gave her a militant glare. "If you accept Lord

Perth's offer, we shall sport a whole new *wardrobe* each, not just a new gown."

Guilt stabbed Joanna in the heart. "I wish I could accept his offer, but it is wholly against my principles. He shan't buy me. Besides, as you well know, Toby will come to his senses. I wish Lord Perth showed some confidence in him."

"I'm sure that ninnyhammer Drusilla Brownstoke has agitated Lord Perth to act on her behalf. That woman has windmills in her head," Oddy said with lively disgust. "It's a wonder that Toby turned out so easygoing and full of pluck. Drusilla has the personality of a ruined soufflé."

Joanna chuckled. "Don't work yourself into high fidgets. Drusilla Brownstoke is not worth your anger. She is a most disagreeable person, but you'd better ignore her—like she does us."

"Oh Joanna, how can you remain so calm when the whole village shuns us?"

Joanna shrugged. "I can't spend my life feeling bitter. As long as we're left in peace, I will ignore the snubs."

They arrived at Marsdon Hall in time for tea. Mrs. Dibble had made scones, and just as she set the plate on the table beside a bowl of strawberry jam, someone banged on the front door. "If that is Lord Perth, we're not at home," Joanna said to the cook. She poured the tea as Mrs. Dibble went to the door. Joanna listened tensely to the voices in the hallway. Drawing a sigh of relief, she recognized Toby's cheerful tenor.

"Are you going to tell Toby about Lord Perth's offer?" Oddy demanded.

Joanna wrinkled her brow. "No, I don't see what I will gain from that. I don't want to come between Toby and his uncle—even if Lord Perth deserves every ounce of Toby's contempt."

"Oh, Joanna, you're too stubborn for your own good. You will drive us all to the brink of despair."

Joanna experienced a sinking feeling in her stomach, but she felt confident that they would somehow prevail financially. In the face of adversity, it helped to keep a level head.

"Dearest Joanna," Toby greeted, and kissed both her hands. "I have missed you sorely, and when I heard in the village that you had taken a drive without me, I was fairly crushed."

"Hmmm, how very thoughtless of me," Joanna replied with a rueful smile. "We had quite an adventure. We met the most ravishing creature that would have spoken deeply to your manly heart."

His eyebrows rose in surprise. "I say! Who was it? I know the village hostelry is overrun by mamas and nubile daughters awaiting a chance to encounter my uncle. Mother is besieged with pleas for invitations to Musgrove Manor. Can't recall I saw anyone even remotely pretty, though."

"A local miss. I'm alluding to Miss Rushton."

Toby plunked himself onto a chair and accepted a teacup from Aunt Oddy. "Oh *her*. She's naught but a hoyden and a shrew. Why, she rides her blasted—forgive me—dashed horse at all hours of the day."

"You don't like an accomplished horsewoman?" Joanna asked dryly.

"We have been at loggerheads for years. Nothing has changed. Annabelle is still an incorrigible tomboy." With practiced ease, Toby scooped up two warm scones and spread them liberally with jam.

Joanna exchanged a merry glance with Oddy. Toby had recovered his good humor after the episode in the boat, and his appetite—if it had ever been lost. "I believe you would find her exceptionally intriguing, Toby. She's a lady who shares your high spirits and love of horses."

Outraged, Toby dropped the scones onto his plate and stared at his beloved. "How can you speak so callously when you are the lady of my heart? You have crushed me, Joanna."

"I beg your forgiveness, Toby. I didn't mean to crush you," Joanna said to soothe the sudden tempest. She could barely suppress her mirth. She changed the subject. "By the way, I saw your uncle down by the lake this morning."

Toby's eyes brightened. "What did you say to him? He came home in a rare taking. I don't think I've ever seen Uncle Terence so ill-tempered. He gave me the most blistering of set-downs, and I don't know why. Called me a bacon brain and a counter-coxcomb."

Joanna could not smother a smile. "And what did you call him?"

"I could not think of anything fast enough. He stormed into the study and slammed the door. There he will brood for the rest of the day, no doubt."

"I told him he was trespassing."

Toby chewed on the scones thoughtfully. "Usually he's rather level-headed, but I believe you've gotten off on the wrong foot with him. I shall induce him to invite you over for tea. That should smooth any ruffled tempers."

"Heaven forbid. He'd rather be pierced with a sword than invite us to tea."

"Hmmm, it's clear you don't know my uncle well. He's a very forthright person, and invariably polite to the fair ladies."

Polite? Joanna shuddered, praying that Toby would forget all about a tea party at Musgrove Manor. If he didn't, she would have to tell him the truth about Lord Perth's bribes. She abhorred the thought of ruining Toby's high regard for his uncle, but it would serve Lord Perth right to have his black heart revealed to his young nephew.

Six

"Uncle Terence, you must see that it is the polite thing to do. Miss Warwick's reputation won't smear off on you. A tea party for your neighbors is de rigueur."

Sitting behind his desk in the study at Musgrove Manor, Terence observed his earnest nephew and seethed inwardly. The cawker was deeply in the throes of calf love, and it was nauseating to behold. If only he could rant and rave at his young relative, but that would only push Toby toward the inevitable—a speedy marriage to Miss Warwick.

Terence didn't doubt for a moment that the tea party was her idea. She'd try anything to worm herself into his household for whatever favors she thought he could bestow upon her. Did she expect him to whitewash her reputation? It was an outrageous thought. To watch Toby make a fool of himself over a brazen hussy was more than enough. Clamping a mental vise around his swelling wrath, he forced a smile to his lips. "Toby, I'm not sure that Miss Warwick will accept an invitation from me. She seems rather a proud female."

"She is proud, and I admire her strength." Toby sighed and clutched his curly head as if plagued by a headache. "Of all my relatives, I thought you would be the most likely to accept my beloved. After all, you have broad views on most issues. When you know

Joanna better, I'm sure you'll see her sterling qualities and understand that she was falsely accused of seducing Leslie Frinton. I'd do anything to restore her reputation." He got up from the wing chair by the desk and started pacing the floor.

"Do sit down, nephew. I don't want you to tear a hole in my carpet with your pacing." His request fell on deaf ears. Evidently Toby listened only to his own inner monologue.

Terence leaned back in his chair and wondered how to best make Toby see reason. "Miss Warwick seems like an agreeable female." *She's vicious, rude, and stubborn,* he added silently. "But I wouldn't rush into Parson's Mousetrap if I were you. I would wait some years before setting up my nursery, spend time in town with my cronies. It's not normal the way you mope about Hasselton, mooning after Miss Warwick. You need some company your own age."

Toby flung himself back onto the chair. "I understand your reasoning, Uncle, and I appreciate your concern. At this point, however, I'm perfectly happy staying on in the village." He gave his Uncle a frown. "Besides, Joanna is not yet in her dotage."

"But the Season is underway in London, and you should be there, paying court to all the debutantes."

Toby gave an exasperated moan. "Why all this talk about the Season when all I asked was that you invite Joanna to tea?"

Terence sighed. Toby must somehow see for himself that Miss Warwick would not do. If only the hussy would accept the five thousand pounds he'd offered, he could tell Toby that his beloved could be bought. But the trollop was holding out for a greater sum. Well, she would have to wait for a long time. He wasn't about to offer more. Five thousand was a small fortune, and the fact that she'd been able to turn down the money baffled him no end. He rose and stretched, easing the tight muscles of his back. "Very well, if you think she'll accept, I shall send her an invitation."

Toby gave a whoop of delight. "While you're about it, you might as well send her one for the ball."

Annoyed, the viscount held back any show of emotion. "I shall direct my secretary to do so. Don't expect she'll accept. The other guests will give her the cold shoulder, and I don't think she's willing to go through such an ordeal. It would be a mortifying experience."

Toby rubbed his hands in evident anticipation. "All she needs is an invitation from someone as influential as you to bring her back into society. Joanna is pluck to the backbone. I doubt she would be mortified by the other guests' treatment."

"Then why has she buried herself in the country all this time?" Terence scrutinized Toby's face, watching the grin stiffen on his nephew's lips.

"I daresay she finds the countryside more rewarding than the city. Gardening is her greatest joy, after all. Anyway, we'll be there to prop her up if someone treats her rudely."

"Ah, the innocence of youth! Always the optimist. It's clear you've been spared the humiliation of a public snub, Toby. I think you won't find Miss Warwick as ready to believe in the kindness of humankind."

"Uncle, you're turning into a bitter old curmudgeon, just like Great-grandfather McBorran."

Terence grew cold inside, and he barely could prevent himself from shaking his irreverent nephew. "Don't speak to me about your libertine great-grandfather. I won't have his name spoken in my house."

"I don't understand your display of animosity toward Great-grandpapa. He's always been a fellow of famous wit and style."

Terence got up and gripped the lapels of Toby's coat. "When have you been in contact with McBorran?"

Toby reddened and wiggled out of his uncle's grip. "I

say! You don't have to strangle me." He gave Terence a furtive sideways glance. "You can't forbid me to correspond with the old codger. He's always been kind to me, and most attentive to my progress at Oxford. Not that I had the bright intellect of a scholar, but McBorran was dashed proud of me." He straightened his coat and fingered his cravat gingerly. "I'll never forgive you if you ruined my neckcloth. Took me two hours in front of the mirror to get the knot just right."

Terence could not quite suppress a laugh. "I hope Miss Warwick appreciates your efforts to appear at your best in her parlor."

Toby's smile returned. "Nothing but the best for my dear, sweet Joanna."

Sweet? Until she has your ring on her finger perhaps, and your purse strings in her greedy hands, Terence thought wrathfully. *Then she'll show her true nature.* He said, "Your devotion commends you. I hope the brightness of your flame will not scorch you in the end."

"Joanna wouldn't do anything to hurt me," Toby replied with great conviction.

Terence said nothing, only went to the door resenting the fact that Miss Warwick would soon sit at his table, eating his widely-liked brandy-flavored cake.

Joanna accepted the invitation to tea knowing that her acceptance would rile the viscount. He inspired her basest instincts, and she constantly caught herself plotting further annoyances for her neighbor. Ever since Lord Perth had moved next door, her tiny world of peace had crumbled. Since their last confrontation, she'd been angry for days, and she was angry now as she turned the gig onto the meandering drive leading to Musgrove Manor. Three days had passed since their quarrel on the lakeshore.

Beside her sat Aunt Oddy, dressed in her finest—if

unfashionable—blue muslin dress printed with sprays of pink flowers, and chatted as if this was the most exciting day in years. Perhaps it was. Aunt Oddy was a social creature, and their confinement at Marsdon Hall must be chafing on her nerves.

"I declare, I'm surprised how rapidly the viscount has improved the grounds," Oddy commented. "The weeds are all but gone, and the new flower borders are already thriving. Not that the plants are flowering. That would be to ask too much, but next year they will blaze with color." She patted Joanna's arm. "Not that his garden will ever be such a paradise as yours. The grounds are much too vast for that."

"I daresay he has a legion of gardeners to tend the grounds. I do everything myself," Joanna said huffily.

Oddy gave her niece a stern glance. "Jo, I beg of you to be on your best behavior. It won't do to completely alienate the viscount. Why, he would see us out of our difficulties, would you but let him."

"I will not discuss the viscount's bribes further. It's wholly against my better judgment to attend this tea party, but I didn't want to disappoint Toby. He's been very kind to me."

"Yes, Toby is a fine young man. I wish you would accept his offer of marriage if you can't accept the viscount's 'bribe.' " Oddy paused, pursing her lips. "I do find it ramshackle of Lord Perth to buy you off, but *five thousand pounds!* Anyone would be a fool to turn away the solution to all our problems." She stuck her nose in the air, and Joanna gritted her teeth. Her aunt would give her no peace, not with such a golden carrot dangling in front of her face.

When she pulled Daisy to a halt outside the marble front steps, she noticed two Indian ladies in saris coming from the lake carrying baskets on their heads.

"Oh my, you could have knocked me over with a feather when I saw those creatures," Aunt Oddy whispered as she stepped up to the entrance behind Joanna. She pressed her hand to her heart as if to curtail its wild race. "How the viscount lives with such strange creatures is beyond my comprehension."

"To him they are not strange. You have to remember that, Aunt Oddy."

"One might just wonder if the viscount is a good *Christian*," Oddy whispered.

Joanna smiled grimly. "If you care to insult him, you'll have your opportunity to ask him in a few minutes."

"Dear me, no. I have no intention of crossing swords with His Lordship, but one *wonders*, you know."

The viscount came out of the study to greet them. He looked handsome and correct in a striped waistcoat and an exquisitely tailored coat of blue superfine. His cravat was tied in the Oriental style, and his wavy hair brushed to a shine. Against her will, Joanna admired his elegance.

"Good afternoon, Miss Warwick, Miss Turnbull." He kissed each hand in turn, and Joanna snatched away hers before his lips touched her skin. Her heartbeat sprinted uncomfortably, but she told herself it was due to her simmering anger, not to any other emotion. Since he had greeted them so cordially, she would make an effort to treat him graciously in return.

The butler was another "foreign creature," to use Aunt Oddy's expression, but Joanna quite liked his white turban and dark almond-shaped eyes that twinkled at her in appreciation.

"I see that you've met Premwar. He's a native of India and speaks English perfectly, if you need to address him," explained the viscount.

Premwar bowed and walked soundlessly across the checkered marble floor. Joanna noticed that his feet were bare except for rope sandals, and his jubbah sparkling white and without a wrinkle. He had an air of peaceful dignity that she seldom saw in the British. Not that she'd studied her peers at close range since the scandal with Leslie Frinton, but—

"What do you say, Miss Warwick?"

"Ah—eh? I'm sorry, I was woolgathering. I failed to hear your question."

"Since the weather is so benevolent, I've arranged for tea on the lawn. I hope you don't mind." Lord Perth smiled, but the smile had an edge to it.

"Of course not. It was kind of you to invite your neighbors," Joanna said with poisonous sweetness. She wondered if he'd invited anyone else, but she doubted it. After all, he couldn't very well mix the pariah of society with the upstanding citizens of Hasselton. It simply wouldn't do.

"What a lovely rose arbor," Oddy exclaimed. "Look Joanna, I'd say he has as many rose varieties as you do."

"I'm partial to roses, and I'm eagerly awaiting their flowering." The viscount threw Joanna a probing glance. She could have sworn she saw a malevolent glitter in the dark depths. "It seems we share an interest, Miss Warwick."

"Probably the only one we share, and thank heavens for that," Joanna replied uncharitably.

"Joanna! That was a cruel observation." Aunt Oddy began fanning herself agitatedly.

"I mean to have the finest garden in the area by next summer," he said in challenge.

"It takes much longer than a year to bring forth such splendor," Joanna replied.

"Not if I have expert advice from my . . . neighbors."

Explosive silence hung between them, and Joanna stared at him suspiciously. She couldn't read his expression clearly, but his voice held a note of honesty. Was he holding out an olive branch to her? Her heart fluttered, and a veil of confusion fell over her mind. She couldn't think of a neutral reply.

Aunt Oddy oohed and aaahed when she clapped eyes on the lavish display of cucumber sandwiches, tea cakes, custard tarts, cream-filled eclairs, and sugar-glazed brandy-flavored cake. The table was covered with starched white linen and matching napkins. An arrangement of hothouse roses in a silver epergne acted as centerpiece. The silverware was polished to dazzle the eye.

"I'm sorry I'm late," Toby cried from the terrace. He vaulted over the low marble balustrade and strode into their midst. His hair was disheveled as if he'd ridden hard. There hung a slight odor of horse about him. "I was delayed at home, but here I am." He gazed deeply into Joanna's eyes and kissed her hand tenderly. He held it much too long, and Joanna noticed the thunderclouds gathering on his uncle's brow. Toby made a handsome leg in front of Aunt Oddy, who laughed and lightly slapped him with her fan.

"You are an impudent charmer, aren't you, young man? I wish I were thirty years younger."

The viscount growled something to Toby, who hurriedly pulled out two chairs for the ladies.

Joanna gave her young admirer a sweet smile and pressed his hand. "Thank you kindly, Toby."

He beamed, his eyes shimmering like stars. Joanna glanced casually at the viscount and got showered with contempt in return.

Terence wished he could rip out that lying strumpet's heart and feed it to the dogs. Still, he couldn't understand why Toby's adoration would annoy him like this. He should not be angry, only exasperated. No female of his acquaintance had riled him like Miss Joanna Warwick did.

Terence was keenly aware that Toby was still holding Miss Warwick's hand.

Toby said, "Uncle, I forgot to tell you that Mother is on her way here. I thought this would be an excellent spot to introduce her to Miss Warwick. I didn't mention that Joanna would have tea with us, only that I had a special surprise for her. She was all agog with curiosity."

Terence's heart sank. *The damned fool!* he thought, wondering how to avert imminent disaster. If Drusilla found the hussy here, heads would roll. He couldn't say anything to Toby about his pact with Dru.

"Oh, she is, is she?" he said casually. "I'd better go and meet her on the front steps." He hurried toward the terrace, but he was too late. His sister's voice already warbled right outside the terrace doors, and Premwar was following her like a silent shadow. The butler gave his master an apologetic look as if he knew about the disaster about to unfold. Premwar had an uncanny knack for predicting the future. He also seemed to read minds, and Terence wasn't sure how he felt about that. Nevertheless, Premwar was an honest and loyal man, and an outstanding servant. But not even Premwar could avert this disaster.

"Theeeere you are, dear brother. I thought that perhaps too much sun had put you to sleep on the lawn." She gave a trill of laughter at her own witticism and fluttered an ostrich fan in front of her face. She wore an unflattering puce gown with flounces that were exceptionally ill-suited to her plump figure. "I didn't know you had planned a tea party." Her gaze swept over the assembled guests, and her smile drained from her face.

"Drusilla, let me explain." As she started to sway, he took her elbow in a sturdy grip and forced her through the French doors and into the relative coolness of the drawing room. She fluttered into one of the chairs and her arms fell lifelessly over the arm rests.

Premwar remained a silent shadow right inside the door, and Terence asked for smelling salts. He sank to one knee and started chafing his sister's pudgy hand. "Don't fly into a pet, Dru. There's no reason to swoon until you've heard the whole of it."

Drusilla opened one eye a fraction and studied Terence from between her spiky lashes. "I've been nourishing a viper at my bosom. How could Toby do this to me, bring me to suffer the darkest depths of humiliation in *her* company." Drusilla moaned and flung her head back against the chair. Fighting a burst of anger, Terence got up and fanned his sister's face with her own fan.

"Come now, collect yourself. I can't very well show my aversion for Miss Warwick to Toby. That would ruin the whole plan, don't you see?"

She opened the other eyelid a crack. "I thought you'd dealt with that matter already. After all, you're not a man to let grass grow under your feet." She fumbled in her reticule for a handkerchief, but Terence pressed his white folded square into her hand. She dabbed at her eyes.

Premwar returned with a bottle of smelling salts, and Drusilla clutched it with both hands as if it were the only buoy in a stormy sea. The butler shot an inquiring glance at Terence, who nodded. "Tell the others to start without us. Tell them we'll join them shortly."

The butler left and Terence watched his sister inhale the acrid smelling salts. Her pasty white complexion took on a healthier glow, and she seemed to be struggling to compose herself.

"Is this part of your scheme?" she asked in a wavering voice.

He nodded. "Yes, I think it is good to know your enemy." He wasn't about to tell her that Miss Warwick had refused his offers of money, and that she was a singularly difficult female. "Please trust me. I know what I'm doing."

"Oh dear, oh dear." Drusilla wiped at her eyes, but Terence could see no evidence of tears. "I don't understand why you would have to put me in this difficult position." She heaved a quivering sigh. "I don't know if I have the fortitude to share a tea table with that *female* and her aunt. 'Twill be the end of me."

"Nonsense!" Terence took his sister's arm and pulled her out of the chair none too softly. "Let's stand together in this. We'll extricate Toby from Miss Warwick's web, and then you'll be able to say you had a great part in freeing him."

Drusilla's eyes kindled with a warlike light. "Well, since you put it in those terms, I guess I can't refuse to help my poor lamb." She straightened her back and righted the black ostrich feather in her turban. "Let's make Toby see the truly wicked side of that Warwick woman's character."

"I hope you'll show some finesse, or the whole event might turn sour and thrust Toby more firmly into her net."

Drusilla marched on. "Don't you worry your head about me."

Filled with misgivings, Terence led his sister outside.

Seven

Joanna watched as her neighborly enemy crossed the lawn with a plump dowager on his arm, Drusilla Brownstoke, the most bigoted busybody of Hasselton village. She had never been a friend of Joanna's, but their neutral relationship of times past had deteriorated beyond redemption after the Leslie Frinton scandal. Ever since, Mrs. Brownstoke had made it her sacred mission to stay away from the inhabitants of Marsdon Hall. Joanna grimaced inwardly, sensing that Mrs. Brownstoke would ring a peal over her head because of Toby's infatuation. She knew she shouldn't have accepted the tea invitation. She had sensed it would be an occasion for disaster.

There was nothing she could do to evade this encounter except bolt across the acres of lawn to the copper beeches that separated Musgrove Manor from Marsdon Hall. But she remained seated. *I have enough backbone to face that old biddy,* she thought, and squared her shoulders mentally.

Anyway, Mrs. Brownstoke looked battle-weary, unsteady on her pins, and her complexion held a distinctly green hue. Joanna exchanged a troubled glance with Oddy. Her aunt's chin had taken on a decidedly hostile set.

"Ah, there you are," Mrs. Brownstoke warbled with

a sugary smile. "Toby, you didn't inform me that Terence had invited more guests to his tea party."

Toby rose and beamed a smile as his mother settled her plump form on a chair by the table. Notably, a chair as far away from Joanna as possible.

"I thought it would be a wonderful surprise for you, Mother. I was sure you've been chafing these many weeks to meet my intended."

A strangled sound came from Mrs. Brownstoke's throat, and she fanned herself frantically. "I'm overset with momentous surprise, my lamb."

Toby's face darkened with sudden mortification. "Mother, please don't call me *that*. I'm not tied to your apron strings any longer."

Mrs. Brownstoke blinked hard at her rebellious *lamb*. She did not reply, only turned a predatory eye on Joanna. "Well, Miss Warwick, how is your gardening progressing? I hear you stay occupied from April to October with your outdoor chores." Her voice took on a hint of evil. "It's commendable to keep one's hands from being idle, don't you agree?" She snapped her fan shut and placed it on the table beside her cup.

"You're correct, Mrs. Brownstoke. Gardening is not for idle people." *Like yourself,* Joanna added silently.

"*I* would not care to have my hands tainted by soil, even though my roses are some of the finest in the region. My gardener—"

"Mother! You ought to see Joanna's rosebushes. They carry hundreds of buds, and I'm certain that any of hers would rival your best."

Mrs. Brownstoke raised her three chins, which quivered with outrage. "I'm certainly impressed by your knowledge of roses, my lam—dearest Toby."

The viscount sat on the opposite side of the table, and the conversation lagged as an Indian servant girl in a maid's uniform served the tea and passed around platters of sustenance. When everyone had helped themselves to cakes and sandwiches, she returned to the house.

"About roses," Toby said, after expertly downing an eclair in two bites. "Mother, between your garden and Joanna's, I believe we shall have a wedding flanked by the loveliest flowers the region can produce." Toby gripped Joanna's hand across the table and gave her an impudent grin. "I do hope you and Mother will put your heads together and plan for the upcoming nuptials. Just as soon as I'm of age, we shall have the banns read."

Joanna forced herself to return his smile. Evidently, he'd not accepted her rejection in the boat, and she feared she would have to banish him completely from Marsdon Hall unless he understood that she would not marry him. But she couldn't very well berate him at this moment. She didn't wish to humiliate him, especially not in front of his mother.

Mrs. Brownstoke gasped for air and looked like she was about to fall into a swoon.

"Toby, the roses might not all be flowering at the time of your wedding," said the viscount, and stirred his tea. At first he'd looked worried, Joanna thought, but now his eyes glittered wickedly.

"The spring has been exceptionally warm. They will flower," replied Toby with the supreme confidence of youth.

"I will not have all my roses cut and despoiled in one day," Mrs. Brownstoke said, enunciating every word. "You have to see reason, Toby."

"Mother, I've always harbored the belief that my wedding day would be the happiest day of your life. You've told me that so many times. A few roses shouldn't be missed."

Mrs. Brownstoke leaned back in her chair, panting, and fumbled for her fan on the table. Aunt Oddy leaned over and slapped the fan in the other woman's hand. A smile softened Oddy's bellicose expression, and she said proudly, "Toby's and Joanna's nuptials will certainly be the happiest day of *my* life."

"No wonder," whispered Mrs. Brownstoke through stiffened lips, "Toby is bringing two hundred thousand pounds to the union."

Joanna experienced a rising anger at Toby for his belief that she would change her mind about his proposal of marriage. How could he tell the world that they would be wed even though she'd refused her consent more than once? As soon as she got a chance, she would have to speak sternly to him. She glared at him, but he refused to heed her anger. The blissful grin could not be removed from his face.

"Mother, I can't repeat enough times how delighted I am that you're finally getting to know my intended better. I'm sure you'll become the greatest of friends." He turned to the viscount, who was chewing a cucumber sandwich and apparently enjoying the spectacle at the table. "Don't you think that in time Mother and Joanna will become bosom bows, Uncle Terence?"

"I daresay they have a lot in common," Terence said, and looked at Joanna from under hooded eyelids. "Both have the most firm opinions on many subjects—especially on the issue of propriety."

Joanna wished she could rake her fingernails across his grinning face, but unfortunately they had been worn down to the quick by constant gardening. "What is proper for one person might be inappropriate for another," she said tartly. "What about bribes, for instance? So many officials and gentlemen are prone to succumb to the vice of greed."

Mrs. Brownstoke recovered enough to sit up straight and speak in a strangled voice. "Bribes? What in the world is Miss Warwick talking about, Terence?" She flattened her hand against her plump chest as if to steady her heartbeat.

Joanna sent a poisonous glance at the viscount. "Unscrupulous behavior, Mrs. Brownstoke," she said. "It is rampant these days."

"Bribes at the right moment have been known to open the right doors," Lord Perth said, unperturbed.

"And elicit the right promises," Joanna added, seething with fury. He had the gall to speak of the subject as calmly as you please, while she'd had the unpleasantness of staving off his aggressive offers of money. "Unscrupulous behavior. I can think of nothing more repulsive than bribery."

Mrs. Brownstoke bristled, her chins wobbling pugnaciously. "If bribes could buy one *peace of mind,* I suppose I would consider it a useful tool." She fixed Joanna with a frosty eye. "In your position, Miss Warwick, I would think that bribes would be the only means to secure invitations to society gatherings—if I may be so frank. After all, everyone knows that you've been excluded from the society of your peers. A lady in disgrace." She took to whipping her fan back and forth in a righteous manner. "I can't pretend that you're other than that."

Joanna pinched her lips shut. She wouldn't rise to the insult.

"It was none of Miss Warwick's doing," Aunt Oddy said, and slammed her teaspoon down on the china saucer.

Mrs. Brownstoke sniffed. "You would be sure to defend your own kin, Miss Turnbull, but I know the truth. Any amount of whitewashing won't change Miss Warwick's reputation." She raised the teacup to her lips and sipped.

"*Mother!*" exclaimed Toby, making his mother flinch as if slapped. She shrieked as tea sloshed over her hand. Toby took the cup from her and set it down. "I have a splendid idea. You're correct that Miss Warwick's reputation is somewhat tarnished—not due to any fault of hers, of course. But you could be of help, dearest Mother. You could show the world that you care nothing for Miss Warwick's status in society, and invite her to your ball. If anything, your taking her under your wing will help to break the ice with the gentry. Joanna will be invited everywhere."

Mrs. Brownstoke paled to the color of starched linen, and the viscount chuckled. Joanna seethed in silence and contemplated leaving the table. This was too humiliating to bear.

"Sweetest lam—Toby, you must understand that my guest list has been carefully arranged. Any sudden changes would overset the delicate balance."

"I'm sure—"

"Toby!" Joanna said sharply. "I'm not interested in attending the local balls."

Toby sent her a crestfallen glance. "I'm saddened by your reaction, my dearest. 'Tis not seemly that you continually hide away in your garden. After all, it would be my greatest joy to introduce you to my friends and relatives."

Mrs. Brownstoke moaned like a cat in pain and pressed a handkerchief to her face. She leaned back in her chair, inhaling great gulps of air.

Joanna dabbed at her mouth with her napkin and put it down with finality. "Toby, I—we have important things to discuss. Don't rush ahead of yourself."

"What *things*?" the viscount asked sotto voce. "The size of your allowance once the nuptials are completed?" He lowered his voice to a whisper. "Believe you me, Miss Warwick, there will be no wedding."

"None for you, maybe. If I were a young lady of sensibility, I would give you wide berth," Joanna retorted in an equally soft voice, "despite the spoils you brought from India." She gave him a withering stare. "I'm sure you acquired the habit of bribing whilst you were there.

Well, it shan't work with me. Toby, I demand to speak with you privately," she added, and rose.

Toby didn't seem daunted by her sharp tone. "Any time, my sweet." He turned to his uncle. "Anyway, you, Uncle Terence, might extend an invitation to your do next Saturday. Mayhap your invitation list is not as rigidly planned as my mother's."

Before the viscount could throw a veiled insult at her, Joanna got around the table and rapped her beau's arm with her folded fan. "Toby, please."

He had risen when she did, but he was reluctant to head toward the house with her. But at her stern glance, he changed his mind and followed her.

"No unwed *lady* would seek a private interview with a gentleman," Mrs. Brownstoke uttered under her breath, but loud enough for all to hear.

Bitterness filled Joanna with a tide of bile. She would always remain an outcast. Sometimes she was able to forget her status of disgrace, but at occasions like this, no one would let her forget. Toby had put her in an intolerable position, and it made her lash out at him just as soon as they entered the drawing room.

"How dare you speak as if we're promised to each other! I've told you in no uncertain terms that I have no intention of marrying you, and I don't understand why you can't accept that, just as I don't understand how you can pretend that we are about to tie the knot. To suggest that your mother should include me in her guest list is bad *ton*, especially when you know how she feels about me."

He hung his curly head, and a stab of guilt went through her. She steeled herself against it.

"I thought Mother would see reason. Your place is by my side, and hers."

"That is *if* I had accepted your proposal, which I didn't." When Toby was about to sink down on his knee, she pulled him upright by the back of his collar. "*Don't* propose again. I'm out of patience with you."

He clasped her hands to the region of his heart. "Oh my dearest, don't crush me like this."

"Cease the histrionics, Toby." She tore her hands away. "I have no other avenue than to bar you from my door."

"No! You cannot be so cruel. I shall wither away with sadness at your refusal."

"Don't be ridiculous!" Joanna stormed out of the mansion. Not waiting for Aunt Oddy to join her, she rushed across the lawn and in among the copper beeches. Her heart was pounding wildly as she reached the back door of her home. Not since the Frinton scandal had she felt such mortification. Mrs. Brownstoke would make sure no one in the area sent out invitations to Marsdon Hall.

With a sob, Joanna sat down on the top step and stared into the green sun-dappled shade of the trees. She wished she could have maintained her composure, but Toby's latest attempt to propose had unsettled her beyond control. Now Aunt Oddy had to face Mrs. Brownstoke's scorn without support, and had to ride home alone.

Joanna propped her chin on her knees and gazed with eyes aching with unshed tears at her peaceful garden. Tuppy—or was it Penny?—joined her on the steps and meowed. She stared with her wise green eyes at Joanna's wet face, and reached up to touch a paw to her cheek.

Joanna laughed through her tears and scooped up the cat, who settled on her lap with a purr. "You don't judge me, do you, Tuppy? Not like people."

The cat yawned with majestic unconcern, displaying her set of sharp teeth and pink tongue.

"Yes . . . you're right. Nothing to bother my head about. Are you advising me to forget the fiasco altogether?" She almost expected the cat to nod her head, but the feline only gave another tremendous yawn and kneaded her paws against Joanna's knees. "I take it that's an affirmation." Joanna kissed the furry head and dried her tears with the back of her hand. Nothing had changed, not really. It was only an incident, and she was safe now. What galled her most was not Mrs. Brownstoke's bigotry, but the viscount's glee. He had no right to laugh at her expense.

The tranquility of the garden seeped into her, and she leaned her back against the door frame. Birds gave a symphony for her benefit alone, and the bees wheeled lazily around her, trying to discover if she carried nectar in one of her pockets. Here was normalcy and happiness, all given freely and without the bite of human narrow-mindedness. One could learn a few things from God's creatures. . . . Joanna dozed as tension slowly left her body.

She awakened as she heard hoofbeats around the corner. The gig headed toward the stables that were partly concealed by a dense lilac hedge. Aunt Oddy had returned, and Joanna was sure that her aunt would be in a state of high dudgeon. If there was a woman Aunt Oddy could not abide, it was Mrs. Brownstoke.

Joanna smiled at the thought of Aunt Oddy at loggerheads with Toby's mother. She was convinced that Aunt Oddy had not restrained her verbal—

He was here. Joanna heard his voice. Her thoughts came to an abrupt end as she realized that Aunt Oddy had not returned alone. She was accompanied by Lord Perth.

Joanna gasped, agitated now that her enemy had pursued her right into her garden. He laid eyes on her just as she was about to get up and rush into the kitchen. Tuppy jumped off her lap with a plaintive meow. The furry traitor greeted the newcomers as if they were her best friends. The cat rubbed against the viscount's leg, but when she discovered that Siddons was perched on his shoulder, Tuppy rushed off, her tail fluffed to double size.

"There you are, Jo," greeted Aunt Oddy. She was flushed, and the embers of battle still glowed in her eyes. "Lord Perth drove me home even though I assured him I could very well handle the ribbons myself."

"I know you're quite the coachman, Aunt Oddy," Joanna mumbled in response.

Oddy snorted and went inside. "I need a glass of water."

"I thank you for your thoughtfulness, but I'd prefer to be alone now, Lord Perth," Joanna said stiffly as her aunt closed the door behind her.

Siddons chattered in recognition and held out her hairy arms to Joanna. The monkey puckered up her lips and tilted her head to one side. Without a flicker of hesitation, she jumped into Joanna's arms, and Joanna couldn't very well fling the animal aside. The monkey was wearing a red sequined silk vest, and a high-crowned hat on her head. Her eyes held real affection, which could not be said about her master. His eyes were as frosty as chips of ice.

"I take it my tea cakes were not to your liking, Miss Warwick." He placed his hands on the small of his back and stared down at her along his nose.

Joanna caressed the monkey's sinewy arm. "There was nothing wrong with your tea, Lord Perth, but your company—well, that's an entirely different matter."

His lips twitched upward. "I found your sparring with my sister rather amusing."

"So you would, perverse man that you are. I'm not surprised that you have only Siddons to call your friend. But then again, she's more accepting than any human being."

His lips widened into a smile as he watched the monkey pull out a strand of hair from her chignon.

"Yes . . . Siddons is quite taken with you, Miss Warwick. That is more than I can say for my sister. Your presence turned her world topsy-turvy."

Joanna started walking along the path that led in among the copper beeches. "You're the only one at fault. I had no desire to meet Toby's mother."

He followed her. "I understand that. You want to tie the knot first so as to silence any protest on my sister's lips."

Joanna's anger rose a degree or two. Let him think that she was a ruthless hussy! She faced him on the path. He was so close behind that she could see the glow of wrath in his eyes. "That's right. Why rock the boat before I have led Toby down the aisle? That would be singularly dim-witted." She forced out a laugh. "You must admit that Toby cuts a most dashing figure. I couldn't wish for a more splendid suitor."

He said nothing to that, but she noticed a muscle working furiously in his jaw. She continued in among the trees while Siddons chattered in her ear. The sun created a golden shimmer among the greenery, and Joanna felt as if she'd entered an enchanted place. If it hadn't been for the irate viscount behind her, she would have thoroughly enjoyed her walk.

"I envisioned that Mrs. Brownstoke's rejection would force you to reevaluate your decision to marry my nephew. She can be very difficult, and she'll see to it that you're excluded from all society functions here and in London."

"I'm sure she will, but I am not marrying *her*, only her son."

"Evidently you don't care a fig for Toby's position. If you're snubbed by all your peers, he will be too. He'll be a prisoner tied to you."

"The veritable ball and chain," she chided. How could he think so lowly of her? All because of an old scandal. "Toby once told me that you are the most fair-minded person he knows. How could he be so blind? You've judged me without caring enough to hear my explanation of the scandal that ruined my life. Toby would be sadly disappointed if he knew the truth about you and your bribes."

"He will never know, because you'll take the five thousand pounds and send him on his way. I know your sort."

Joanna stopped abruptly, and he bumped into her from behind. To prevent them both from falling, he gripped her shoulders. She could hear his angry, agitated breathing close to her ear. His hands burned her through the thin muslin of her sleeves. She gasped, standing perfectly still. He stood as if paralyzed, then he slowly turned her around on the path. She faced him, hot mortification surging into her cheeks. They stared at each other for the longest moment. Every sound had receded to a whisper, even Siddons's continuous chatter. As the viscount pulled Joanna close, the monkey jumped up into the branches above.

Joanna could see every line in his face, every nuance of expression moving in his eyes—anger, confusion, pain, and finally wonder. As if in a trance, he lowered his mouth to hers and kissed her as she'd never been kissed before. A wave of bliss rolled from the top of her head to the soles of her feet. She lost her grip on reality as his kiss burned her, his tongue making lacy circles around her own. His mouth claimed her very life force, pulling her essence into himself and giving her his. Filled with an urgency she could not explain, she clung to him. His strong arms encircled her waist, one hand moving up her spine, caressing. She melted, filling with a glowing warmth. Her heart raced, her skin tingled, her very soul cried out for him.

When he straightened his back and gazed down into her face, she thought she would swoon at the sultry heat in his eyes. His hard face had softened and was diffused with desire.

"Why?" she whispered, unable to pull away from his embrace.

Her word broke the spell, and he let go of her abruptly. His jaw set in a hard line. "I . . . I thought I'd taste the pleasures that sent Toby into such transports of bliss. After all, I needed to know your secret weapon that holds my nephew captive."

Her golden glow evaporated like an elusive cloud of perfume. His kiss had only been part of his campaign to destroy her connection to Toby. She should have known. "Let me tell you, Lord Perth, your kiss, compared to Toby's, was disgusting. Kissing a toad would have been preferable."

Eight

Toad! Terence knotted his hands into fists to stop them from grabbing and shaking her until her teeth rattled. He put as much boredom into his voice as he could muster. "I take it you practice daily on toads to get the right slithery touch." He felt an urge to run from her, to get away from her accusing eyes.

Two red spots glowed on her cheeks, and Terence found himself longing to pull her back into his arms and kiss her until she had no fight left in her body. Never had he experienced so many conflicting emotions: anger, exasperation, helplessness, and—yes—desire. He gazed at her, wishing she wasn't such a schemer, such a grasping hussy. Sunlight pierced the dense foliage above and streaked her hair with gold. Her skin was luminous, roses and cream, and he yearned to trace his finger along the graceful contours of her face. Her eyes were blazing sapphire magnificence, and her lips soft and vulnerable—so eminently kissable.

"Why, I don't need toads. I practice on any suitable male present." She nipped around him on the path. "Good day, Lord Perth. If you think you've humiliated me, you've failed miserably."

He watched her back, stiff with anger, as she hurried down the path toward Marsdon Hall. An intense warmth blossomed for an instant in his chest, but he concentrated on his wrath. An idea was slowly forming in his head. What if he could make her fall in love with him? Then she would get rid of Toby. After all, if the schemer was after a wealthy husband, he had much more to offer than Toby. He could court her, put all his charm into play and see where it would lead. He could keep himself detached, only work toward freeing Toby from her. His anger would make him immune to her wiles. If he succeeded, it would be a glorious day when he could jilt her. That would be the perfect lesson! A small voice inside reminded him that it would be an ungentlemanly thing to do, but he silenced the protest with a vengeance.

Delighted to have found a possible solution to the problem of Toby's entanglement, Terence called to Siddons and headed out of the woods and across the lawns of Musgrove Manor. The seduction wouldn't cost him a groat. . . .

He entered through the terrace door. The servants were in the process of clearing off the tea things, and Premwar hovered in the hallway. The monkey jumped onto the Indian's shoulder.

"Did Mrs. Brownstoke leave?"

"Yes, my lord, Mr. Toby conveyed her home."

As Terence was about to enter his study, the butler cleared his throat. "My lord, a letter arrived while you were gone."

Terence lifted his eyebrows in inquiry and took the note from the silver platter. Sitting down behind his desk, he cracked the seal and spread the paper. It was from his grandfather, McBorran. He stiffened, and filled with dismay, he read,

Grandson,

I hear that you have returned to your country of birth, a move that delights me more than I can say.

I feel my end is near, and I would like to make peace with you before I go. I'll arrive at Hasselton on the twentieth day of June, and will take a room at The George. An excellent hostelry, I hear. There I will await your invitation to Musgrove Manor. I cannot die in peace if we don't settle our differences.

Y'r affectionate grandfather,
McBorran

Dread spread to every part of Terence's body at the thought of having to see his grandfather after so many years. It was to get away from McBorran and his debauchery that he'd left in the first place. Terence crumpled the letter into a ball and threw it across the room. Brooding, he leaned his head into his hands and propped his elbows on the desk. He'd had nothing but difficulties since returning from India. First Toby and Drusilla, now this. Perhaps his decision to come back had been a mistake. He had cut off all contact with McBorran, and he liked to keep it that way. His grandfather only brought the more painful memories of his mother. He could not bear to remember her betrayal.

"Damn it all to hell!" he swore, and slammed his fist into the gleaming desk top.

It was in a foul mood the bailiff found Lord Perth when he entered five minutes later carrying the estate ledgers.

The following week, Joanna and Oddy tooled the gig down to the village for spools of thread and a tin of China tea. The sky wore a cloak of sullen gray clouds, and rain was imminent. "You'd better hurry with your errands, or we'll be drenched before we reach home," Oddy said, glancing suspiciously at the sky. "I'll wait in the gig."

Joanna entered the only shop in the village that sold everything from milliner's supplies to garden rakes. When she returned with her purchases, she found Oddy conversing with an old gentleman dressed in elegant if outmoded garb. His silver hair waved back from a high forehead and his face held deep lines of dissipation. He had once been a handsome man, but his broad shoulders now slumped tiredly and his eyes were rheumy and bloodshot. He lifted his hat to Joanna and bent his tall frame into a graceful bow. There was something familiar about his face, but Joanna could not make the connection.

"Good afternoon, miss," he greeted in a warm if raspy voice. "I was just asking for the direction to—"

"Mrs. Brownstoke's house," Oddy interrupted. Her voice was clipped and cool, but her face held the flushed look of excitement. "This is the Earl of McBorran, Mrs. Brownstoke's grandfather. He's come down from the north to visit."

"Oh," Joanna said with a flare of curiosity. The viscount's grandfather as well as Drusilla's.

His blue eyes twinkled at her, and Joanna was aware of the abundance of charm he'd once possessed, and still did, but in less dazzling shades.

"This is my niece, Miss Warwick, the mistress of Marsdon Hall."

"I'm enchanted to find such glowing beauty hidden in these rural parts of England. I see that my stay at Hasselton will not be a waste of time."

Silver-tongued devil, Joanna thought, charmed, though, against her better judgment.

"I thought that Lord McBorran—if he doesn't mind troubling himself—would like to come to tea tomorrow," Oddy said. Joanna studied her aunt's face thoughtfully. Shut away from society, Oddy was increasingly lonely in the old mansion, and any stranger visiting was like a fresh breeze in their confined lives.

"I think that's a splendid idea," Joanna said, wondering if he knew about her status in the village. "How about four o'clock tomorrow afternoon?" She smiled at the old gentleman, thinking he might fail to appear once he heard about her disgrace. Someone at the inn was bound to inform him if he divulged that he'd been invited to Marsdon Hall.

"I humbly accept," he said with another bow. "Four o'clock." He gave Oddy a dazzling smile and sauntered down the street.

Oddy stared wistfully after him as Joanna jumped into the gig. "What an old scoundrel, but a charming one," she said with a sigh. "Perhaps it's never too late to fall in love."

"Oh, Auntie, you can't fall in love in five minutes," Joanna scoffed.

"Who's to say? Five seconds is enough if the right gentleman enters your life." Aunt Oddy stared after Lord McBorran until he stepped into the local tavern, The Old Smuggler.

They purchased the tea and turned Daisy toward home. By the time they had reached the outskirts of the village, it started to rain. Joanna, who was controlling the reins, urged Daisy on, but the old nag had difficulty stretching her stiff legs into a gallop. When they neared the gate at Marsdon Hall, they were overtaken by a lady on horseback.

Joanna recognized Miss Rushton. The young woman shouted a greeting, all the while shielding her face from the pelting rain.

"Come with us to Marsdon Hall until the storm moves away," Joanna cried over the noise of the downpour.

Annabelle flashed a grateful smile and galloped through the open gates. She slid from her horse and led it into the stables, then returned to help settle the gig in the carriage shed next to the stables.

"Thank you," Annabelle shouted as they ran up the brick path to the house. "I would have been drenched to the bone if I'd continued all the way home."

They shook out their damp skirts and cloaks in the kitchen, and Mrs. Dibble threw her hands in the air as she viewed the soggy crown of Joanna's bonnet. "Your hat is ruined beyond repair, Miss Warwick. Whatever shall I do with it?"

"Don't worry your head over it. Tea, please, Mrs. Dibble, and scones in the parlor," Joanna said, and ushered her guest through the house.

"Make yourself comfortable, Annabelle." She motioned toward the worn sofa and shivered with cold. Rain sluiced against the windows, and the room was as dark as if evening had arrived. She lit kindling in the fireplace to chase off the damp chill in the room. When the kindling had caught, she settled two logs on top, then sat down in the wing chair close to the warmth.

"It's very cozy in here," Annabelle said, casting shy glances around the room.

"Kindly spoken," Joanna replied with a smile. "It is, however, rather a cave than a palace."

"It reminds me of home. We—ahem—aren't very well off, just like you, and—" She blushed and bit her bottom lip as she searched for a way out of her gaffe. "Oh dear, I'm frightfully sorry."

"Don't be." Joanna laughed ruefully. "You're right, I'm poor, and I'm afraid that—" She didn't have time to finish her sentence as furious pounding sounded on the front door. "What in the world—?" She rose, smoothing her damp hair, and walked to the hallway. Coming from the kitchen, her aunt reached the door first. She opened it a crack, and a gust of rain-filled wind tore inside.

"Toby! What are you doing outside in this weather?" She opened the door wide enough to let the young man through. "You're as wet as a frog in a pond."

He shook himself like a dog, scattering waterdrops in all directions. When he laid eyes on Joanna, he gave a strangled cry. "My dearest! I have been unable to sleep since our last confrontation." He stood in front of her, a hangdog expression on his face. "Say that I'm allowed to see you again. I promise I won't embarrass you with offers—"

"Toby!" she admonished, and placed a hand on his arm. "I told you in no uncertain terms—"

"Please forgive me. I can't bear the thought of never visiting you again. I won't embarrass you."

Joanna's resistance wore down. "Very well, we're just about to have tea. Please join us."

His face broke into a sunny smile. "*Thank* you, Joanna, I knew you would relent. You have much too soft a heart to harbor a grudge."

"You're right in that, Toby," Oddy said with a sniff. "Her heart is much too soft for cheeky rapscallions like you. Take off your wet coat and hang it out here. No need to stain the upholstery with water."

He bent down and planted a kiss on Oddy's temple, and the spinster blushed with embarrassment. "You young so-and-so."

Joanna led the way back to the parlor, closely followed by Toby. She smiled at Annabelle, who wore a frown on her face.

Toby stopped as if suddenly turning into a statue on the threshold. His eyes widened, and displeasure replaced his erstwhile smile. "Miss Rushton, what are *you* doing here?"

"What kind of greeting is that, Toby?" Joanna admonished.

"Don't worry about us, Joanna. Toby and I are not polite with each other. Stems from the fact that we've hated each other for a long time." She turned to Toby. "Isn't that so, Toby?"

"Hate is a very strong word," he said, evidently hesitating whether to remain in the house or bolt out the door. "Rather strong dislike, I'd say."

"I won't tolerate any mud-slinging in my house," Joanna said sternly, while recalling the time of her heated argument with Toby's uncle. She leaned back in her chair and watched her beau as he chose to sit on a chair as far away from Annabelle as he possibly could. "Why are you hostile toward one another?"

Toby and Annabelle exchanged glares, and Toby reddened. "I—well, perhaps we shouldn't talk about that now."

"Tell her," Annabelle challenged.

Toby cleared his throat, his face filled with misery. He was saved, however, by Mrs. Dibble who carried in the tea tray, followed by Oddy bearing the kettle.

Annabelle smoothed back her hair self-consciously, wreaking more havoc to her damp blond curls than the rain had done.

Besides anger and hurt, Joanna sensed a more deep-seated pain in her young guests, and she was intrigued. What had caused the rift in their friendship?

"How is your mother?" Aunt Oddy asked Toby as she served the tea and passed along the cups. Mrs. Dibble had failed to produce scones, but there was a fresh spongecake to offer their guests. Joanna watched the meager fare with misgiving, wondering if she would be able to afford many more spongecakes in the future.

"Mother could not be in better fettle," Toby said briskly, but Joanna heard the false note in his voice.

"I thought the tea party taxed her beyond endurance," Oddy said with a sly wink at the young man.

He shifted uncomfortably. "Mother is easily overset. The smallest things send her off into the boughs." He accepted a slice of cake with alacrity.

Annabelle's eyes lit up with curiosity. "You met Mrs. Brownstoke, Joanna?"

"Yes . . . as a matter of fact, we collided on Lord Perth's turf."

Annabelle gasped and clapped her hands together. "I wish I had been there to witness one of Mrs. Brownstoke's swoons."

"I'm sure you would have enjoyed it no end, Annabelle," Toby said acidly.

"Don't say you haven't noticed your mother's expert swoons, Toby," Annabelle scoffed.

"She's not strong. She has spells of dizziness."

"Oh, pooh, only when it suits her."

Joanna broke in. "Perhaps we should not defile someone who is not present to defend herself."

Annabelle gave a trill of laughter. "She would rather be dead than set a foot in this house. You might as well be aware of that, Joanna."

"That's enough!" Toby rose, his cake plate falling to the floor and scattering crumbs over the carpet. "You're greatly exaggerating things, Annabelle. As usual."

"You have spoken quite frankly, Miss Rushton," said Oddy. "But I'd rather you did not. I can't abide bickering, and you're heading toward a full-fledged fight with Toby."

Annabelle lowered her eyelashes and blushed. "I'm sorry, Miss Turnbull. My temper always gets the best of me. Mother is quite distraught. She says I'll never fix Lord Perth's interest if I don't curb my temper."

"Fix Terence's interest?" Toby stared goggle-eyed. "He's old enough to be your father! You're excessively muddle-brained if you believe for one second that you'll be able to catch his attention. Why, he'd rather marry a—a sheep than you!"

"At least he has some sense in his head, something you lack sorely. Anyway, if I don't marry Lord Perth, Mother will force me to wed an acquaintance who is older than Methuselah."

"Your just desserts," Toby said scathingly.

"What did Miss Turnbull say? No arguing in this house," Joanna reminded them.

Toby couldn't take his eyes off Annabelle's flushed face, and he was breathing hard through his nose. *For once I'm not the center of his attention,* Joanna thought, amused. Her spirits that had been sagging at the thought of Toby's relentless pursuit lifted a notch. If she nudged the two young persons in the right direction . . . who knows what might come out of it?

Nine

Wearing her dingy gardening smock over her dress, and a dilapidated straw hat, Joanna went outside the next morning. Raindrops from the showers on the previous day glittered on every leaf and flower, and puddles glistened in the sunlight. The air held the fresh scent of a newly scrubbed world. The tang of wet soil lifted Joanna's spirits as she gathered her tools. After pulling on stout gloves, she pushed the wheelbarrow that held spade, hoe, rake, and various plants, along the meandering brick path at the back of the house. She would weed the flower borders while the soil was loose after the rain, then plant the seedlings in her rock garden.

The sun warmed her back and made perspiration bead on her forehead, but that didn't stop her from extricating stubborn dandelion roots from a row of peonies. Despite the heat, it was work that took her mind off her problems and filled her heart with contentment.

She worked through the morning. Before long, the sun had crept high in the sky, and it was time for the midday meal.

Straightening her back, Joanna admired the weed-free border. Besides the birdsong, the air seemed alive with noises, among them, the crunching of many carriage wheels over gravel. She shaded her eyes and glanced across the copse of beeches. Her neighbor's drive was full of carriages of all shapes and sizes. Amazed at the cavalcade, Joanna watched young ladies in pastel-hued morning gowns and chaperones in more somber colors enter the manor house. What in the world was the viscount up to now? A daytime ball? There was no such thing, she concluded, therefore the ladies must be morning callers, or maybe there to attend a picnic by the lake. She spied Drusilla Brownstoke's barouche, and realized that Toby's mother must be acting as the viscount's hostess. Evidently all of Drusilla's acquaintances with nubile daughters in tow had descended on Musgrove Manor.

Joanna smiled in glee as she pictured the viscount doing the pretty to all those females. His patience must be sorely tried. It was clear that Drusilla had plans to marry off her brother to the most eligible of Sussex's young ladies.

"Well, whoever is foolish enough to become his bride is welcome to him," Joanna said between clenched teeth. He'd been nothing but a thorn in her side, but perhaps that would change. Marital plans might be just the thing to make him forget his campaign to ruin her life.

Joanna trembled with a surge of anger, but she also remembered their heated kiss and the hot desire that had engulfed her at his touch. She'd tried to suppress the memory, but it crept up on her when she least expected it. At night in her dreams, during the quiet time when evening arrived each day, in the middle of a meal, it sneaked into her mind. In fact, she had not much control over her emotions, and the memory had been nagging her sorely during the last few days. She had reveled in the kiss, but also felt shame that Lord Perth had thought so little of her to take advantage of her. It reminded her of Leslie Frinton and the shame that went with that recollection. No man was ever going to make a fool of her again, and if Lord Perth ever tried to kiss her again, she would slap his face.

She watched as Aunt Oddy trudged down the path bearing a bouquet of hothouse roses of the palest pink hue. They were lovely, and Joanna wondered who'd sent them. Lord McBorran? He was coming to tea, and Oddy wore an air of excitement. Penny and Tuppence, two plume-tailed gray shadows in her wake, halted when they came eye to eye with a teasing flycatcher on the lawn.

"I'm ever so curious to learn who sent these to you, Jo," Oddy said, panting with the exertion of hurrying across the yard.

"For me? Who in the world would send me roses? I thought they were for you."

"Perhaps Toby. The footman who delivered them wore Perth livery." Oddy thrust the flowers at Joanna, who inhaled the sweet fragrance of the barely opened blooms.

She stiffened as she studied the gift, sensing that Toby was not the giver. "Perth livery? Why would Toby send over flowers from Musgrove Manor?"

"Well, they have a large greenhouse at the manor. Read the note."

Joanna pulled off her gloves and extricated the folded missive and broke the seal. She scanned the lines. "These roses remind me of the pink flowers in your cheeks after our delightful kiss. Perth."

Crumpling the note convulsively, she felt heat rise in her face. It would not do for Aunt Oddy to read the provocative words. She glanced at her aunt's round face, noticing the question in her eyes.

"Well? From Toby?"

Joanna nodded, unable to find her voice. She looked away as anger flared in her chest. What was Lord Perth's game now? Was he going to torment her for succumbing to his embrace? The very nerve of the man!

Aunt Oddy sighed and put a hand to her heart. "He's a romantic young man, and so taken with you," she said. "I wish I were twenty-five years younger."

"You're most welcome to him," Joanna said coldly, while contemplating whether to put the roses on the compost heap or in a vase. "I've told him not to press his suit."

Aunt Oddy wailed. "I despair of you, Jo. Has your heart grown so hard that a gentleman's love cannot touch it?" She gave Joanna a rebellious glance. "To be frank, I'm sorely disappointed in you. I always thought you had inherited your mother's tender heart and sweetness of disposition."

Guilt washed through Joanna, and she gave the bouquet to her aunt. "I'm sorry if I sound callous, but I don't love Toby, and he knows it. I will not pretend otherwise. Please put these in water for me."

Aunt Oddy dithered, holding the roses as if they were as fragile as a newborn babe. "Well . . . you could always try to love him. Why, my hair is turning gray what with all the problems heaped upon our heads. Toby would *take care* of us." Tears made Oddy's eyes brighter, but she struggled valiantly not to cry.

Joanna's spirits sank. Had she been wrong not to take Lord Perth's offer to save Aunt Oddy this pain? No. She pushed aside that thought in a hurry. She would never stoop to taking bribes. And now, what plan had evolved in his devious mind? The gift of flowers had taken her completely by surprise.

After chasing off the bird, the cats wound around her legs, meowing to get attention. Joanna lifted one of them and stroked the silky gray coat. "Go inside, Auntie, I'll follow shortly. And don't worry. We shall come about somehow."

Aunt Oddy left without another word. Joanna had an

impression that the roses wilted already, just like her aunt. She had to come up with an acceptable solution to lift them out of their impoverished state.

She glanced across to Musgrove Manor and fought an urge to stalk over there and slam her hoe through one of the windows, preferably the room where the viscount was holding court with the ladies.

She sighed and let the squirming cat down. A cup of tea was what she needed more than anything.

When she returned outside, the sun had disappeared behind a bank of clouds. A dense blanket of humidity had replaced the freshness of the morning. Hornets buzzed angrily around the flowers as if irritated by the change of weather. Joanna pulled on her gloves and retrieved the hoe that she'd leaned against the wall earlier.

She surveyed her haven, the masses of flowers in bud. Perhaps she could sell some at the market later in the summer, or trade them for victuals. It was something to think about. . . . Her gaze wandered across the yard and came to rest upon a figure standing silently amidst the copper beeches.

Her breath catching in her throat, she stared at Lord Perth, because it was him, looking splendid in buckskins and a superb double-breasted frock coat of brown cloth. The starched neckcloth was a study of artful folds, and the beaver hat sat at a dashing angle on his dark head.

Most of all, Joanna noticed the warm smile on his face, and it made her hackles rise. A fox's grin. His unexpected appearance was just another part of his devious game, she reasoned.

"Well, well, I see that my warning has fallen on deaf ears," she said, and stalked up to him. "I mean it, Lord Perth, I shall report you to the law for trespassing."

"There's no hurry, surely," he drawled, and took off his hat. He threaded a hand through his hair, and Joanna felt a disturbing flutter in her stomach as if he'd touched her. "I needed a stroll, Miss Warwick, and I saw you through the trees."

"I did not invite you," she said, her voice faltering. "Besides, I don't understand why you seek my company. You have professed to loathing my presence."

He glanced at her for a long moment with unsettling dark eyes and twirled his hat between his hands. "I think our last meeting changed all that."

Joanna's heartbeat speeded in a most wanton fashion, and she was glad she was wearing an all-concealing smock lest he notice her palpitations. "Nothing has changed. You should not have sent me flowers."

"My dear Miss Warwick, how graceless you are. Why not accept a gift from an admirer? Let us form a truce."

Joanna inhaled sharply and clutched the handle of the hoe until her hands ached. "Admirer? Does that mean you have changed your opinion about me, about my reputation?"

He strolled forward and she noticed the sudden heat in his eyes. "Some ladies can't help their passionate nature, and mayhap you're one of them."

Joanna swallowed her rising anger. His gaze mesmerized and confused her. "So now you've come to take advantage of what I so freely give to gentlemen? Is that it?" She slammed the hoe into the ground, right in front of his toes. "There's no measuring stick long enough to measure your conceit, Lord Perth. If you think that a bouquet of roses will pave the way for your seduction, you're more mutton-headed than I thought possible."

The warmth in his eyes cooled considerably. "I could do without your tongue, Miss Warwick. It's best put to use in a more silent, more . . . intimate manner."

"I've had enough of your insults, milord. Get off my land." Joanna turned on her heel and ran back into her garden. Her emotions in a muddle, she wished she had never laid eyes on the viscount. How could he be so rude and treat her as if she were a strumpet? Did he ever question his own judgment? Evidently not. Not only was he a boor, but an idiot as well. Tears blinding her eyes, she began hoeing another flower border. She sensed that he was still there, staring at her back. Tears rolled down her cheeks, but she swore she would not let him witness her distress. She gulped down a sob and swallowed the salty flow of her tears.

She heard his soft steps on the grass and stiffened.

"I told you to leave."

He halted beside her. She kept her head bowed and looked at the mellow sheen of his much worn topboots. She wasn't going to give him the satisfaction of seeing her tears. Then a pristine handkerchief entered her vision as he thrust it toward her.

"I'm sorry," he said.

Silence stretched taut between them. Joanna finally snatched the proffered white flag and pressed it to her face. It smelled faintly of leather, and of *him*. She blew her nose in an unladylike fashion and gulped down a few more sobs.

"I truly am sorry," he continued. "Even if you were a lady of the night, I have no right to treat you so rudely."

"I suppose that's what you think of me," she said to the handkerchief. "A tart."

"Well, prove to me otherwise. The world—including my sister—has branded you a wanton, but I'm willing to listen to your explanation."

"How magnanimous of you," she said, her face still buried in the handkerchief. "I don't have to explain myself to you." She glanced up at him, not caring any longer that her eyes would be red with tears. "In fact, I don't give a fig for your opinion of me." She inhaled a trembling breath. "If you want me to accept your apology, you have to accept me without any explanations."

His lips quirked upward at the corners. "You drive a hard bargain, Miss Warwick."

"Actually, I don't need your friendship, Lord Perth. I have known others who accept me the way I am." She went to the wheelbarrow and placed the hoe among the other tools. She longed to get away from her annoying neighbor, but at the same time, she was reluctant to go.

He spoke to her back. "Toby thinks so highly of you that I realized I'd better find the Miss Warwick who has bewitched him. Most certainly she's not the harpy I have come to know."

Joanna heard the sincerity in his voice, and she wondered what had made him change his tune so completely. Surely not the kiss . . . She felt weak and defenseless, emotionally tired. She looked long and hard at him, noticing the candor of his expression, but she decided not to trust him entirely. After all, this might be just another feint in their battle.

He swept out his arm. "Your garden is lovely. Soon the green will be intermingled with all colors of the rainbow."

"Flattery will not get you what you want," she said darkly. She pushed the wheelbarrow toward her new rock garden, and he followed.

He fell into step beside her. "Tell me, Miss Warwick, do you know what I want?"

She stopped and faced him. "I have my suspicions. But let me inform you, Lord Perth, that I'm far from the innocent miss that was taken in by Leslie Frinton."

"I'm sure you are," he murmured. "But—" He didn't finish the sentence, only reached out and dragged one long finger along her cheek.

She flinched away and went to stand on the other side of the wheelbarrow. "If you are a friend of Toby's, and his guardian, why do you treat me like this? Toby would be very upset to know that you sent flowers to his intended."

She noticed the flush rising in his cheeks and the flare of embarrassment in his eyes. "I touched a raw nerve, didn't I, Lord Perth? Why go behind Toby's back?"

"My being here has nothing to do with Toby, Miss Warwick. If you love him—like you say you do—my presence does not change that fact. He has nothing to fear from me."

"Still, you're acting without his knowledge. Would you dare to tell him that you sent me roses and a provocative note?"

He shrugged carelessly, but Joanna sensed his uneasiness. "No need to alert Toby. *You* are the one to make the choice between us."

Joanna's jaw dropped. "Are you offering me the same as Toby . . . marriage?" She stared at him in confusion, unable to read his, by now, closed face.

"Perhaps. If you're willing."

He could not mask the indifferent tone of his voice, and Joanna's anger rose. "You don't love me," she said heatedly. "In fact, you loathe me. You have no intention of offering me your name. This is just another chapter of your nefarious schemes."

"Overly suspicious as always, Miss Warwick. Why do you only see the baser side of my nature?"

"Because there is no other side." She gripped the smooth handles of the wheelbarrow and continued toward the rock garden at a good clip. "Good day, milord. We have nothing more to say to each other, and from now on, I wish that you stay away from me."

She arranged her tools on the ground and studied the design of the rocky mound. She'd decided to plant iberis in one corner. With any luck, next year the area would be glowing with tiny white blooms. Ignoring the approaching man, she sifted the peat on the tray containing plants and pulled out some root stock. With a trowel in her hand, she sank down on her knees ready to loosen the soil for planting.

"No need to be so brusque, Miss Warwick. We have much to discuss."

She gritted her teeth as she compared the viscount to an annoying hornet. "I have nothing else to say to you."

He got down beside her, his knee landing clumsily on top of one bare iberis root.

"Look what you did!" Joanna shouted, and motioned him aside with her trowel. With a moan, she retrieved the crushed root. "This won't grow now."

"Just plant it, and we'll see." He took the root from her, and the trowel. "I'm not wholly inexperienced in gardening matters."

Seething, Joanna watched as he flung soil in all directions with the trowel. "Be careful! I don't want you to ruin my other arrangements."

"It's a bit late in the year to start planting," he commented archly, and stuck the root in the ground.

Joanna could not suppress a laugh when he left the wrong end sticking out of the soil he'd packed around it. "Experienced gardener, you say?" She calmly took the tool from him and gently dug the root out. As he watched, she turned the stock, leaving the end that had the beginnings of bud above ground. Not that it was easy to see which end was which.

He cleared his throat, evidently embarrassed. "I was going to turn it, you know."

"Of course you were." For a moment, Joanna forgot her anger and luxuriated in the pleasure of having company in her garden. Since Aunt Oddy had no interest in plants, Joanna spent long hours alone. Now a very virile—if obnoxious—gentleman knelt so close to her that she could smell the spicy fragrance of his shaving soap.

He gazed about him in wonder. "Do you know the names of all your plants?"

"Yes, I do. Before I decide to introduce something new, I learn everything about the plant's care first."

"Very impressive." He sat down in the grass, his thigh brushing against hers. She moved aside quickly, but she'd already absorbed the hard muscular feel of him.

"I've planted creeping phlox and sedum at the other corner. I'd like to find some dwarf asters to plant for the fall, but I've not been able to locate any."

"Perhaps my gardener can help you. I'll ask him."

Joanna didn't know how to respond to his sudden kindness. When they didn't argue, he seemed a different man. "I take it gardening is not one of your interests, Lord Perth. Do you care for any other pastimes?"

He pulled a blade of grass from the lawn and chewed on it. "I collect rare books, especially illuminated manuscripts, and since I lived in the East, I find exotic spices and teas interesting."

"Toby told me you're a connoisseur of teas. He prefers China tea, as do I."

"You have not had the opportunity to taste the many varieties available, but I'm importing different kinds, from China and the island of Ceylon. I predict that India tea will be all the rage."

"Toby mentioned it."

He frowned, his eyes full of suspicion. "What else has Toby gossiped about? Mayhap you know more about my life than I know of yours."

"But you know all that's *pertinent* about me, don't you, milord? What else of interest is there?"

"Am I supposed to cringe from the sting of that barb?" He leaned back on his elbows, a lazy smile on his face.

Joanna swallowed hard as she viewed that glorious smile. "If you wish."

"I have no more energy for arguments. Your garden has steeped me in peace. In fact, the air is so somnolent I think I could go to sleep if I were to lie down." He shifted the grass to the other side of his mouth. "What else did Toby tell you about me?"

Joanna made a show of thinking deeply. "He said that you're the best uncle imaginable."

The viscount laughed. "You're very diplomatic."

Joanna decided to pry more deeply. "My aunt, however, heard the gossip that you were jilted in India, not once, but twice. I take it the young ladies found you overly high-handed, annoyingly stubborn, and prone to sudden rages." Unable to hide her smile, she observed the dark clouds gathering on his brow.

"You draw hasty conclusions about my character, Miss Warwick."

"Then we're guilty of the same flaw, milord. I seem to recall that you eagerly embraced society's verdict without forming your own opinion about me."

"You're striking low blows, Miss Warwick."

"They hit home." She brushed some dry soil from her sleeve. "You must admit that your failures in the courtship department have not detracted from your reputation, like my mistake impaired mine."

"I have nothing to be ashamed of," he retorted huffily.

"I'm sure you don't, milord, but why did the ladies jilt you? There must have been a reason. Most ladies I know would not turn up their noses at a title and a fortune."

"You certainly turned up yours at the small fortune I offered."

"Like I've told you many times before, I don't accept bribes."

Silence fell like a heavy blanket over them. He stared at her through slitted eyes, and Joanna felt a warm softness spread through her body. This man was dangerous to her senses, and it would be the height of folly to remain under his spell any longer.

He took a deep breath and spoke. "For your information, I courted the daughter of my partner in Calcutta. Sophie was lovely in a delicate sort of way. I realized later that we would not suit. I like to spend part of my days outdoors, and she abhorred the thought of riding or strolling. When she went anywhere, she traveled in a carriage. Anyway, I was too old for her." He fell silent, then added in an almost inaudible voice, "I could not engage her heart."

Joanna sensed his discomfort. "Someone else did?"

"Yes, a British sea captain, at least seven years my junior, and very dashing. He made me feel old and decrepit."

Joanna sneaked a look at his face, noticing the pain it caused him to speak of his failures. "But you are not very old, Lord Perth."

He chuckled then. "Nor are you."

"Old enough to be considered on the shelf." She pulled off her gloves and righted the straw hat. He made her overly self-conscious, aware of her tatty appearance.

"Well, Sophie was barely nineteen. Too inexperienced for matrimony. Besides, she was dreadfully spoiled."

"You were lucky to be rid of such a ninnyhammer," Joanna said with a chuckle.

The viscount pulled a fistful of grass and threw it at her. She fought an urge to laugh and cry at the same time. The green blades fluttered past her vision, and she dashed them off her smock. She could barely talk for the emotion churning in her chest. "Do be careful, milord. If I wanted my lawn closely cropped, I would employ sheep."

"There were not many eligible British ladies to choose from in India."

Joanna cleared her throat to strengthen her voice. "I take it the rejection smarted?"

"You know how to turn a knife in a gentleman's heart, Miss Warwick."

"He might need to have the knife turned." Joanna called to one of the Persians that was watching them from the brick path. "Cats are more honorable creatures than gentlemen, don't you agree? I know from experience. I would never stick a knife in Tuppence's heart, but you—"

He stared at her intently. "You sound bitter. You're too young to be so disillusioned."

"I lost all of my innocence in one stroke. It took no longer than ten minutes, and I was just eighteen. I've been an old woman ever since."

"Nonsense! You've made a life for yourself here."

Joanna was going to say that young women rarely gardened all day; they were busy in the nursery. But she kept silent. No need to bare the deep well of her humiliation. She had to remain strong for his next attack. If he knew the extent of her vulnerability, he would demolish her in their next battle.

He clearly sensed her distress, because he didn't pry. "I courted another lady, Miss Melandra Brixton, a traveler and a missionary. She was a strong woman, full of zeal and purpose. I was drawn to her individuality and her courage. But she had absolutely no humor. Our union would have been disastrous, and I was relieved when she broke off our engagement."

Joanna detected a false note in his voice, and felt his suppressed pain. It was as if all her senses were tuned in to his every expression, and it frightened her. Why did she have to care about his feelings?

"You . . . sound unhappy," she whispered, unable to stop herself. "You loved her."

He gestured toward Musgrove Manor. "She was a great woman, not like the hothouse flowers my sister keeps parading in front of me. I share nothing with the debutantes of seventeen and eighteen." He gave her an assessing glance. "Why, I share more with you, Miss Warwick, though we're prone to argue."

"I don't usually argue, but with you—"

He sat up and leaned toward her. An intense light shone in his eyes, and she could barely breathe. "It wouldn't have to be like that. We still have many things to discuss, to discover about each other."

"I don't see—"

"I have revealed two painful memories to you, Miss Warwick. I had no reason to do so, but in my willingness to bridge the gap between us, I told you about my failures." He gripped her arm, and his touch seared her like fire, a fire that did not hurt. Quite the contrary. "Now, what are you willing to give in return, Miss Warwick? The sordid truth about your past?"

Ten

Joanna was on the verge of opening her heart and pouring out her pain to the viscount, but if she did, would he believe her? She was so close she could see the emotions shift in his coffee-brown eyes: curiosity, deviousness, eagerness, and, yes, compassion. Fearing the flash of deviousness that might lead to more pain later, she only said, "You already know the version that the gossips have created. Besides me, Leslie Frinton is the only person who knows the truth; he was there. He kissed me, and . . . touched me. My dress was—"

"And you enjoyed it?"

Silence hummed between them, heavy with suggestion.

"Lord Perth, you're acting in a most ungentlemanly fashion. Surely you would not ask one of your lady guests if she enjoyed the caress of—"

"It depends. It's nothing to be missish about."

Joanna laughed incredulously. "Missish? That's ridiculous. A lady in her right mind would not reveal the details of a romantic encounter to a gentleman, let alone her—enemy. Your persuasive talents are sorely inadequate, milord."

He touched her chin with his fingertip, and she flinched back. "We could always make this into a romantic tryst, create our own sweet memories."

"To create more grist for the Hasselton gossip mill? No thank you, Lord Perth. I've had quite enough of that." Joanna rose quickly, before she could succumb to the hot suggestion in his eyes. The last thing she wanted was to fall for his virile wiles.

"You disappoint me."

"And you shock me."

Joanna was saved from further conversation as Aunt Oddy called from the back porch. "Lord Thistlethorpe is here, Jo. He wants to speak with you."

Joanna filled with dread. Thistlethorpe had only one item he wanted to discuss: her marital status and how he wanted to change it. How odd that she would be besieged by two gentlemen in the same day. Lord Thistlethorpe had a stronger argument than Lord Perth, and if she didn't want to become Lady Thistlethorpe, she'd better find a way out of her financial dilemma posthaste.

Lord Perth loomed over her, so close she felt dizzy with his nearness.

"Good-bye, milord," she said, and started walking toward the house. She hadn't gone far before Lord Thistlethorpe came outside and minced across the lawn toward her. He fluttered a lace-edge handkerchief at the flies buzzing around his head.

"*There* you are, my lovely!" He stopped abruptly as he laid eyes on Lord Perth. Raising an eyeglass to his eye, he said, "Well, I'm surprised that you entertain gentlemen unchaperoned, Joanna. Must think of your reputation. Why, I don't want to hear any gossip in the village about my future wife."

"Future wife?" Lord Perth whispered incredulously.

"Don't worry, Lord Thistlethorpe, my companion was just about to leave."

The viscount crossed his arms over his chest and wore a stubborn expression on his face. "Really, Miss

Warwick, 'tis rude to dismiss your guests in such a perfunctory manner."

"Guests, yes, but not intruders."

Lord Thistlethorpe waved his handkerchief in an agitated fashion. "Is he molesting you?" He put a protective arm around Joanna's shoulders, and she felt hemmed in by males on both sides—a stifling experience, to say the least.

The viscount quirked his eyebrows and gave Joanna a teasing smile.

"I'm certain our relationship is in no danger from Lord Perth," went on Lord Thistlethorpe, "but I don't take kindly to interlopers. Miss Joanna is as much as promised to me at this point," he directed to the viscount.

Joanna pulled away as his foul breath washed over her. She could not abide his clawlike touch and possessive demeanor. His presence made her cold inside with worry.

"Have you come to discuss a business matter, or is this a social call?" she asked the old roué.

His seamed face cracked in a devious smile. "I thought I'd better remind you of our agreement. Time passes very quickly."

Joanna folded her hands together. "I have not forgotten, Lord Thistlethorpe. Truly, your offer is constantly in my thoughts." She threw a glance at the viscount and noticed that his gaze had narrowed with suspicion.

"Good, my dear Joanna," said Lord Thistlethorpe. "I know you're a sensible woman besides a lovely one. I expect you to make the right choice." He shaded his eyes and glanced around the garden. "It would be a pity if you were to lose all this."

The viscount had moved closer to Joanna, and she sensed him stiffening at the old man's words. "Lose it?" he asked in surprise. "Why?"

"It's a matter that does not concern you, Lord Perth,"

Joanna said tightly. She turned to Thistlethorpe. "We should discuss this at another time—in privacy."

"I see that we understand each other well, Joanna dear." The old rake gave her a lecherous smile and bowed. "I shall call again *soon*." He left, meeting Aunt Oddy on the path. She escorted him around the side of the house.

Joanna drew a sigh of relief.

"I'm surprised you entertain that old goat in your home," the viscount said hotly. "He's a libertine, or was one, the worst kind of person."

"No reason to fly into a pelter over it. Who I entertain is none of your business."

"Don't bite my head off, Miss Warwick. I ask because I'm concerned."

"Nosy is more like it." Joanna wished he would go away. The heat of the afternoon was oppressive. Thunder hung in the air, and she felt a headache start at the base of her skull.

Aunt Oddy returned, and the sound of a retreating carriage could be heard from the lane. "Lord Perth, do you wish some refreshment? A glass of ale, perhaps?"

He shook his head. "No thank you, Miss Turnbull. I have matters to attend to at home."

"Oh. Your days must be filled now that your grandfather has arrived in Hasselton. He's a delightful man."

The viscount snorted. "So he has already taken you in, Miss Turnbull? He wastes no time. If I were you, I would stay far away from Lord McBorran. He's no better than the libertine who just left."

"Certainly not! McBorran seems a perfectly harmless gentleman. In fact, we've invited him to tea. Should arrive any minute now. Please stay, milord."

"Certainly not! I refuse to see that man," the viscount said with sudden venom.

"Milord! That's no way to speak about your grandfather. In my day, we were taught to revere our elders."

"Be that as it may, but my grandsire is not worthy of my respect."

Filled with curiosity, Joanna stared at the viscount. His eyes smoldered and his hands were clenched into fists. What had happened to create such antagonism between him and his grandfather?

"Well, he's certainly welcome in this house, isn't he, Jo?" Aunt Oddy bristled like an irate hedgehog, and Joanna couldn't help but chuckle.

She addressed her neighbor, whose face had darkened with wrath. "I think my aunt is quite taken with Lord McBorran. I can't very well *forbid* her to see him. I don't try to force people to obey my commands—like certain persons I know." She nudged his arm, and he scowled at her.

The haze had deepened over the area, and the airlessness had expanded, or was it the viscount's intense gaze that made it increasingly hard to breathe? Joanna wondered.

Oddy spoke. "I'm going back inside before the storm arrives. Besides, I promised to help Mrs. Dibble with the sandwiches." She headed toward the house. "Don't dawdle, Joanna," she called over her shoulder.

Joanna felt self-conscious when left alone with the viscount. She picked a piece of grass from her sleeve. "Well, I guess I should gather my tools before I get drenched."

He glanced at the thunderheads on the horizon. His face had lost all its animosity. "If it rains, the old man won't leave the inn," he said as much to himself as to her.

"Why does it bother you so much whether Lord McBorran arrives or not?"

The viscount gave the impression of looking down his nose at her. "You made a mistake inviting him."

She sighed in exasperation. "It's strange that you should warn me against your own grandsire." Before he could answer, she continued. "By the way, why isn't he staying with you at the manor? I find it distinctly odd that he has taken a room at The George."

"He knows he would not be welcome at the manor." Perth gave a stiff bow. "It's time for me to leave."

Joanna smiled wickedly. "Well, for one who wasn't invited, you stayed for a long time."

Eleven

"How very gracious of you to alleviate my lonely sojourn in this part of the country," Lord McBorran said as he viewed his glass of port with delight.

Joanna smiled and topped off the glass. There was not much left in the bottle, the last they had in the house. She prayed it would be enough. Anyhow, Aunt Oddy would enter with the tea kettle any minute.

Thunder rumbled in the distance, and Joanna was glad she'd found time to work in the garden before it rained. However much she'd accomplished was another matter. Most of the time she'd argued with Perth. She looked at the old lord and wondered if the viscount would look like him in his old age; hair turned silver, features honed sharp, and eyes faded and wise.

She smoothed her pale blue muslin gown and was glad that she'd taken the time to rearrange her hair and don her second best dress before the visit. For some unfathomable reason, she wanted to make a good impression on the earl. "I spoke with your grandson—Perth—earlier today in the garden."

The smile on the old man's face lost its brightness. He set down his glass and Joanna noticed that his bony hand trembled. "My grandson . . . what wouldn't I do to speak with him again! I—I don't have too long to live. There's not much strength left in this old body."

"Nonsense. You seem spry enough, milord."

"I traveled south expressly to see Terence, and Drusilla, of course. I cannot rest easy unless I heal the rift with Terence." He brightened as he looked at Joanna. "Mayhap you could help me, Miss Warwick."

"In what way?"

"Speak to him on my behalf."

Joanna leaned back in the sofa and laughed. "You're surely jesting. Lord Perth won't listen to anything I have to say. I might as well make a clean breast of it. Lord Perth and I are enemies."

"Hmm, I know that infernal temper of his is at fault, and he's more stubborn than what's good for him."

"I agree. I'm sorry I can't be of any help, but you must not give up."

He thoughtfully fingered the silver handle of his walking stick. "What have you done to stir his ire, Miss Warwick?" He took a sip of port while peering at her over the gilded rim of the glass.

"He accuses me of seducing Toby Brownstoke." Joanna felt heat rising in her cheeks. She took a deep breath. "You must have heard that I have a tarnished reputation. I'm surprised you would deign to visit us here at Marsdon Hall."

He chuckled and slapped his knee. "When you're as old as I am, you realize that what happened in the past isn't very important in the great scheme of things. Everything evens out in the end." His kind smile lingered. "Miss Warwick, I advise you to find some young man to marry and forget all about your troubles in the past. Marry Toby if that's what you both want. I'm sure you're a lady who would make any gentleman happy. Toby is fortunate if he can kindle your love."

Joanna enjoyed a sense of relief she hadn't experienced for a long time. She quite liked the old man. He had lifted the burden from her shoulders and made her feel unsullied and cherished. "Thank you for your generous words, Lord McBorran. I wish I could help you with your grandson, but any advice I give him, he's likely to throw back in my face."

"Terence's a stubborn young fool!"

Aunt Oddy entered with a tray bearing the teapot and a plate of cucumber and fish paste sandwiches. Mrs. Dibble followed with a basket of shortbread.

Joanna realized she was hungry after her emotional encounter with the viscount. She helped to pour the tea and handed the earl a cup. The cook left and Aunt Oddy sat down beside Joanna on the sofa. She looked excited due to the appearance of their new visitor.

"I wish my grandson would find someone sensible and lovely like you to marry, Miss Warwick."

"He'll soon choose one of the ladies that Mrs. Brownstoke has introduced to him," Aunt Oddy said. "The parade at the manor is endless."

McBorran chortled. "He won't have any of those hen-witted females. He needs a lady with a bit more steel in her backbone. Terence could never abide fawning debutantes."

Strangely disturbed by the talk of the viscount's future bride, Joanna took a sip of tea. "He told me about his failed courtships in India."

"Pshaw, I'm glad they failed! Why should he bury himself at the other end of the world? If he had, I would never have had the chance to see him again. The quarrel would never be resolved."

"What nature of a disagreement?" Aunt Oddy pried shamelessly. "Mayhap I could be of help?"

Joanna gave her a warning frown, but Aunt Oddy held her ground. "Lord McBorran shall tell us everything if he pleases to do so, Joanna."

"I'm afraid it is a long story, as long as my life. But suffice it to say, Terence thinks that I have much too liberal opinions about honor and respectability."

"You seem like a very respectable man to me, Lord McBorran," Aunt Oddy went on.

"You might have sung a different tune thirty years ago, my dear Miss Turnbull. My morals were perhaps not the highest, but I realized I had only one life and wanted to make the most of it. Why, there are tribal men in Africa who have four or five wives without counting that as a sin. I had only one mistress, and Terence has always judged me very harshly for that. He blames me for his grandmother's death, says she died from a broken heart. The truth is that she had an incurable ailment."

Joanna noticed the distress on his face, and she said, "You don't have to explain all to us, milord. I feel that your grandson ought to meet with you and let you clear up any misunderstanding. He owes you that much, doesn't he?"

The old earl hung his head. "*I* owe him, not the other way around." He lifted a trembling hand to his eyes. "There was the matter of my gambling. I don't think Terence will ever forgive me."

"All gentlemen gamble," Aunt Oddy said comfortingly, and put two sandwiches on a plate, which she placed before the old man.

"Yes . . . but not like I did. I was part of the deeper, more immoral gambling of the day. It was like an obsession with me, and I couldn't stop until I had lost everything, *everything*. I don't know how I've lived with myself ever since."

Heavy silence fell, and Joanna moved uneasily on the sofa. She exchanged a shocked glance with Aunt Oddy at the disclosure, then glanced at the earl with compassion.

"Come now, Lord McBorran," Oddy said at last. "We all make mistakes, some greater than others, but that doesn't mean we're lesser beings."

He raised his pained eyes to her. "You're a kind

woman, Miss Turnbull. When one gets this old, one needs forgiveness for past sins. That is all that matters to me now."

The wind rattled the windowpanes and the trees. Rain spattered intermittently against the glass, and thunder boomed overhead.

"Even nature is displeased with me," the earl said quietly, and squeezed the handle of his walking stick.

"Balderdash!" Joanna said. She sensed the depth of his wound. "You must go about solving your problem with confidence. If I were you, I would pester Lord Perth until his resistance breaks down. Sooner or later he's bound to listen to you."

"You're an optimistic lady, Miss Warwick, and full of spirit." His face lit up with a smile. "It's quite contagious, you know."

Mrs. Dibble returned to refill the teapot. She carried a stiff folded note in her hand, which she gave to Joanna. "One of the manor footmen brought this over earlier, but I forgot to give it to you."

"Hmmm." Joanna turned the parchment over and recognized the Perth seal in red wax. "What is he up to now, I wonder?" As the others went through the tea rituals, she opened the missive and read silently.

When Mrs. Dibble had left, Joanna dropped the paper on the table. "You won't believe this, Aunt Oddy, but we've been invited to Lord Perth's great ball."

"Well, he said he would invite us. Rather, Lord Thistlethorpe insisted that we be asked."

"I'm not going, and that's that! It would be stupid to open myself up to snubs and ridicule." Anger and grief warred in Joanna's chest at the thought of the gentry's rebuffs.

"Perhaps the local families have forgotten," Aunt Oddy said gently.

"They never forget—or forgive. I shall not attend." Joanna glanced at the old man on the opposite side of the table. She tapped the invitation thoughtfully with her fingertips. "I have an idea. You, Auntie, shall go and bring Lord McBorran as your escort. Perth can't very well throw you out. It says the Misses Warwick and Turnbull, *and* escort."

Aunt Oddy gave the earl a hopeful glance. "What do you think, milord? It would be an opportunity for you to see Lord Perth. Like Jo says, he can't very well throw you out."

"Oh, I don't know," he said, but Joanna could see the bright hope in his eyes.

"I won't take no for an answer, Lord McBorran. You must take this chance." Joanna forgot her own sorrows as she planned McBorran's entry to Musgrove Manor. It was a perfect way to confront the viscount. One part of her wanted desperately to be there and watch his wrath, but another part was sad that she couldn't attend as an honored guest. She pushed away her lingering sadness. It would not do to dwell on old injustices.

"Lord McBorran, I'm excited about this plan. You must say that you agree to it. On the night of the ball, we expect you to arrive promptly and escort my aunt."

He rubbed the bony knuckles of one hand and two bright spots glowed in his cheeks. "I think it's a capital idea, Miss Warwick. My only reservation is the fact that you won't be there."

"Don't worry about me. I simply would not consider attending." Joanna pushed aside a sharp stab of disappointment. At least she had a chance to help the old man, and that made her happy.

"You're kind and considerate," Aunt Oddy said, and patted Joanna's knee. "But you're much too young to be closed in with us older people. Youth is for gaiety and romance."

"Please let's not talk about me any longer. We must plan our strategy."

* * *

On Saturday, a lovely evening as the sun hung orange over the horizon, Lord McBorran arrived to escort Aunt Oddy to the manor ball. Aunt Oddy had spent hours in front of the mirror, and Joanna had helped her arrange her hair in a becoming chignon adorned with a cluster of ostrich feathers dyed the same dark blue color as her old silk gown that they'd spent hours refurbishing with brighter blue velvet ribbons.

"I feel like a queen," Aunt Oddy wailed as she dabbed some powder on her cheeks as a finishing touch. "But as nervous as a debutante before her first ball."

Joanna laughed and adjusted the long silk gloves on her aunt's pudgy arms. "I darned the elbow, and it doesn't show much. No one will notice in the candlelight."

"You've always been a good needlewoman, Jo. Actually, you're good at just about anything you put your mind to. You always were a fine girl."

Joanna tapped her chin thoughtfully as she viewed her aunt's reflection in the mirror. "I have been busy planning our future this last week. Mr. Hobson at the mercantile has promised to send us provisions in return for fresh flowers from my garden every morning. He can make a profit selling those to the local houses."

Aunt Oddy's eyes sparkled. "What a splendid idea! It means we won't starve in the near future, at least until our vegetables have matured."

"That's right. And I put a notice in Hobson's window that I'll give pianoforte lessons for a fee. That might bring in some funds, maybe enough to buy stuff for new gowns. We need something warm for the autumn."

Aunt Oddy gave her a warm hug. "I could not wish for a kinder or more generous niece. I only wish that you would find a gentleman—"

"No, don't talk about that now." Joanna averted her

eyes. "When you see Annabelle tonight, give her my best, Auntie, and ask her to stop here soon."

Aunt Oddy looked searchingly into her eyes. "Toby will be there. He'll be disenchanted that you're not present."

Joanna laughed. "He'll forget me in time. Make him dance with Annabelle."

"He would rather eat his own hat than dance with her," Aunt Oddy said with a gurgle of laughter.

There was a knock on the door downstairs, and Joanna ran below to open it. The Earl of McBorran looked resplendent in an outmoded brocade frock coat with silver braiding. He wore knee breeches and white stockings. His shoes had silver buckles and the handle of his cane had been newly polished.

"You look exceedingly handsome, Lord McBorran," Joanna said, and held out her hand to him. He bowed from the waist and planted a light kiss on her knuckles.

"And your smile's a sight for sore eyes. I've looked forward to this evening, but now I'm nervous. My grandson will be very angry to see me."

"If I know him right, he won't create a scene in his own home. He has more control than that. But, like you said, his hackles will be up." She laughed. "I wish I could be there to watch."

He cocked his head to one side and winked. "Who's stopping you? You could always hide behind the shrubs and glance through the windows."

Joanna stood on the path among the copper beeches and listened to the strains of violin music coming from the neighboring estate. Ever since Lord McBorran and Aunt Oddy had left, she'd been plagued by a deep sense of sadness. She had been unable to remain in the house with only the cats for company. Waves of music and laughter had prodded her to pace the rooms.

Finally she'd decided to go outside. If she couldn't

attend the ball, why shouldn't she take some small part in it? It wasn't as if someone would be hurt if she admired the latest fashions from London and Paris through the windows.

Taking a deep breath, she hurried along the path. She wore a dark cloak to conceal herself from head to toe. She was certain that no one would notice her as she blended in with the darkness.

Lord McBorran's old traveling coach was one in a long line of carriages, and Joanna wondered how the viscount had taken the shock of meeting his grandfather after so many years. Evading coachmen and lackeys, she crept up to the rhododendrons growing on both sides of the front entrance.

Hiding behind those, she sneaked along the wall and, through the tall windows, had a splendid view of the vast hallway with its curving staircase. Guests in light-hued silk gowns and sparkling jewels were conversing with Lord Perth and Drusilla Brownstoke at the top of the stairs before proceeding into the ballroom.

Even at this distance, she saw that the viscount looked dazed, unsmiling, his sun-bronzed face tinged with gray. Footmen in livery carried wraps and hats upstairs to the ladies' retiring room, and others bore trays on their shoulders.

Joanna saw Toby, elegant in a black cut-away coat and white satin waistcoat, conversing with an old gentleman in an old-fashioned tie wig and knee breeches. Toby kept throwing surreptitious glances toward the door, probably expecting her, Joanna thought.

A twinge of guilt went through Joanna as she watched the viscount's face. She was party responsible for his current misery, but she felt that the old man should have a chance to redeem himself. *Stiff-rumped bore,* she thought as she scrutinized her enemy, but the slur held no depth. Somehow she had come to care for the man even though he had the worst manners possible.

She continued along the wall and wished she could climb upstairs and look through the ballroom window, but she had to be content with the glances she caught of the ladies' finery downstairs. She positioned herself by another window, where she could see the entrance clearly without being seen in return. Carriages were still rumbling up the drive, disgorging guests on the front steps.

Annabelle was one of them, and Joanna recognized Mrs. Rushton, a thin, sallow-faced woman with a bilious expression. Joanna admired Annabelle's gown, a cream silk with a beige lace overlay, short puff sleeves, and pink velvet ribbons adorning the bodice and the hem. With her ringlets piled high and held back with the same ribbons as on the gown, Annabelle would have looked adorable if it weren't for the sullen expression on her face. Evidently, she'd had words with her mother along the road to the manor.

Toby was coming downstairs and stiffened as he laid eyes on Annabelle. Joanna wondered why they shared such animosity, and vowed to find out.

She watched other guests and admired their gowns and jewels. She would have enjoyed wearing such finery, if only once. It seemed so long ago she'd had her debut in London and worn lovely silk dresses and translucent pearls. The pearls had gone toward settling her father's debts.

But she had no regrets, not now. It was true that time healed all wounds. With a sigh she left her hiding place, but she didn't feel like going back to the hall, not just yet. She would sit in a quiet spot and listen to the lovely music flowing through the open windows.

She crossed the lawn and headed toward a wooden bench in the rose arbor at the back of the house. The night seemed dreamy, unreal. The moon came out from behind the clouds and cast a silver sheen on the greenery. She leaned back and listened to the music for a long time, almost falling asleep on the bench.

Suddenly she heard voices close by, and she darted into the shadows before the couple came upon her. She ran down the slope to the boathouse. Waves lapped gently against the shale, and she stepped out onto the dock. Surely, no one would find her so far away from the house. She could still hear the music. The moon cast a lane of light on the water, and as Joanna neared the end of the dock, she stiffened. A dark shape sat dangling long legs over the side. The dock moved as the shape moved.

"Who goes there?"

Joanna recognized Lord Perth's imperious voice and stiffened. What was he doing here?

She debated whether to run away without answering, but he'd heaved himself to his feet before she could turn around. He gripped her arm. He pushed back the hood of her cloak, and she could see the surprise on his face in the moonlight.

"Miss Warwick? What the deuce—?"

"I'm sorry. I shall leave at once, since I'm trespassing." Even if she wanted to leave she couldn't. His grip hardened, and except by creating a struggle, she could not free herself.

"What are you doing here?" His voice held an edge of ice.

"I was taking a stroll and longed to listen to the music. 'Tis very lovely."

"Stop pretending that everything is normal, Miss Warwick," he spat. "I'm well aware that you're responsible for setting me up to meet my grandfather. It was a very sly move, and I admire your gall."

"I take it you're not pleased. You don't sound it." She tried to wiggle out of his grip, but he pulled her closer.

"You think I *should* be pleased? Evidently you know best, as always. What I want is not important, is it? I told you expressly that I had no intention of speaking with my grandfather, yet you contrived to get him into my house."

He stood so close she could smell the wine on his breath and the male fragrance of his skin. "You sent me an invitation to the ball, and since I was unable to attend, I couldn't very well send Miss Turnbull without an escort."

"You knew my wishes, yet you flaunted my grandfather in my face."

She tore away from him as anger rose in a wave in her chest. "You're old enough to confront him, don't you think? Why avoid the problems? Wouldn't you rather deal with them in a responsible fashion? He has a right—"

"I don't know what the old bleater told you, but obviously he has taken you in with his yarns. I thought I could count on you to keep—"

"Count on me, Lord Perth? What have I promised you? We're enemies, and probably always will be. I think Lord McBorran has a right to explain his behavior. He's a frail old man, and wants to clear his breast before he dies."

The viscount seethed in silence, and she knew his eyes would flash fire if she could see them.

"What's so terrible that you can't find it in your heart to forgive him, milord?"

Joanna thought he would push her into the water as he directed his anger at her, but he only sat back down on the dock and lifted his legs over the side. He grabbed a handful from a pile of shale beside him and started skipping the pebbles on the water. Joanna debated whether to leave or stay, but she sensed that he needed company—even if it was her, not his best friend.

She sat down beside him, dangling her legs, too. "I didn't want to play a trick on you, Lord Perth, but the only way you would accept your grandfather's presence was in the company of others. Didn't you feel . . . anything when you saw him?"

The viscount snorted. "Outrage is what I felt. Even as we speak, he's spinning his stories to anyone who wants to listen. As long as I've known him, he has embroidered on the truth."

"I find him charming and kind. Perhaps he stretches the truth a little, but there's no harm in that, surely? I don't understand why you would judge him so harshly for flaunting a mistress—"

"*That* detail might be acceptable," he hissed, "but it's only a small part of his miserable mistakes."

"He told me he had a penchant for deep gambling, and that he regrets his poor judgment in the past. I don't see why that would make you so bitter. My father gambled; he was a disgrace, a complete wastrel, but he never failed to show me that he loved me above all else. Love is what made me whole; love is what made the years of my childhood a bright memory. Perhaps love made me naive. I couldn't understand that some people weren't honorable." She chewed on her bottom lip to gather her crumbling composure. "But I learned my lesson. Bitterness, however, is a disease I fight every day of my life."

He kept skipping stones, listening. Joanna didn't know why she'd bared her heart to him, voicing things that she usually kept hidden.

"You're a paragon of virtue," he muttered scathingly, "at least in your own eyes. That doesn't erase the fact that Leslie Frinton ruined you, and you let him do it. What gently bred *lady* would have sneaked away with a gentleman for a romantic tryst *á deux*? Mayhap your upbringing wasn't all it should have been."

Joanna's voice trembled with anger. "What right do you have to criticize me? Are you so exalted that you can't forgive any blunders, not even those made by your own relatives? Everyone, including you, makes mistakes." She whispered in his ear, "I think your upbringing was sadly inadequate if you can't forgive your grandfather. What did he do to *you*?"

He turned to her and gripped her shoulders hard. "If you must know, Miss Inquisition, he squandered my birthright. He frittered away everything on harpies and tarts, flung the family fortune to the winds during his nights of gambling, and humiliated my grandmother."

"Then he was just like you—thought only of himself."

Lord Perth shook her, but she continued. "McBorran has changed, and you have to forgive him."

He was breathing hard through his nostrils. "As you have forgiven Leslie Frinton for ruining your life?"

"I was a fool listening to his blandishments, but why dwell on past mistakes?"

"That indiscretion has shrunk your world to a dilapidated house, a mountain of debts, and a secluded garden. Don't tell me that you don't wish for more." His face loomed over hers, and she held her breath. His angry eyes held a silver sheen cast by the moon, and his hard grip burned through the material of her cloak. An eager, dangerous voice inside her prayed that he would crush her to him and kiss her until she forgot everything, just like that other time. Another part of her yearned to run away and hide, to protect herself from falling in love again—with a highly unsuitable gentleman.

"I've accepted my life," she whispered. "Even if I am notorious. Still, I don't understand why you would always think the worst of me."

His heated breath fanned her face. "Perhaps I knew someone just like you, someone who flung propriety to the winds. She also flung her responsibility toward her family to the winds. She was no better than the lowliest woman in the alleys of St. Giles."

"Who?" Joanna held her breath, knowing she'd touched a festering wound in him.

His hands trembled around her arms and his voice sounded tortured. "My mother. She left everything behind when she ran away with one of McBorran's grooms. She left not only emptiness, but humiliation."

"Because of my one mistake, you see only her in me. Isn't that so, milord?" Joanna fought an urge to cry as she waited breathlessly for his reply. It came after a long moment of silence.

"Yes . . . but no, not really. You're tempting me beyond endurance." He groaned and clutched her tighter.

"So you feel guilty that you're drawn to a lady of loose morals," she whispered through stiff lips. He didn't reply, only stared at her in the moonlight.

"Forgive her, forget the past and your bitterness," Joanna said when she couldn't bear the silence any longer.

He growled deep in his throat and crushed his mouth to hers. He pressed her back until she was lying on the dock and flattened her with his weight as he explored the tender insides of her mouth. He kissed her like a ravenous man, and sparks of desire shot to life everywhere in her body. Dizzy, she noticed the hair falling over his forehead, and beyond it the blinking stars that serenely returned her dazed stare. Music filled the night and played on her senses, just like the viscount's closeness ravished her sensibility.

She pushed against him, fought with his roving hands until he looked up, a confused expression on his face. "S'faith woman, but you can kiss," he said hoarsely. "I can't seem to slake my thirst for you."

"Please let me up," she begged. "Even if Leslie Frinton had the opportunity to brand me a strumpet, it doesn't mean that I am one. You're not treating me any better than he did, Lord Perth. You've taken advantage of me."

He heaved himself up from the dock, his breath coming in labored gasps. Without responding to her admonition, he pulled her up. They swayed together, and Joanna had to grasp his arm to gain her equilibrium. Tears gathered in her eyes as she studied him. Evidently he thought she was his for the taking.

"I didn't come here to get mauled," she said stiffly as her vision blurred.

He brushed back his hair, evidently struggling to regain his senses. His voice held no emotion as he finally spoke, "You said you learned a lesson in the past, Miss Warwick. Then, what are you doing unchaperoned outside in the middle of the night?"

"My reputation cannot be ruined again, surely, but that doesn't mean you have the right to take advantage of me. I am not offering myself to you." She tore away from him and dried her tears on the back of her hand. She hurried onto the shore and glanced at the brightly lit manor house.

"Wait! I had no intention of pushing myself on you," he called after her. "Our intimate talk inspired me. I'm sorry."

"Don't lie to me! Go back to your guests. They must wonder where you are."

She did not look over her shoulder to see if he had obeyed. Darting in among the trees, she didn't feel secure until she had reached the moonlit garden of Marsdon Hall. Her home lay in complete darkness, but she knew she would have no difficulty finding the sanctuary of her bedchamber.

She could not, however, make herself go back inside. The night seemed enchanted, like something out of a fairy tale, and she wondered what magic had touched her. Surely not Lord Perth's. He was no better than any of the libertines he professed to despise. Yet . . . yet, his touch had ripped her defenses apart, and she felt as if she was bleeding from a wound deep inside. Oh why, oh why, had she been so foolish as to let him kiss her?

Twelve

The viscount heard his sister call to him through the terrace door, but she sounded far away, unreal. Had he only dreamed the enchanting encounter with Miss Warwick? No, her every word stayed as if burned upon his mind. The feel of her lingered in his hands, and the taste of her on his lips. Dazed, he wandered up the slope thinking how different she'd seemed tonight, not at all the reserved lady he'd come to know, but a warm, passionate woman who was lonely. No wonder that Toby had fallen for her if he'd tasted those luscious lips. . . . *Toby*, how was he ever going to convince his nephew to abandon Miss Warwick?

The viscount sighed heavily. He could not loathe her like he had in the past. After tonight, he could almost believe her innocence—that she'd been cruelly used by Leslie Frinton. Yet she returned his kiss wantonly, like someone experienced in lovemaking. He didn't know what to believe. Determined to forget her for the rest of the evening, he pushed away the memory of her sweet mouth.

"*There* you are, Terence. What in the world happened to you? You've been sorely missed by a handful of ladies," Drusilla admonished. She fluttered her hands nervously in front of her face. "It will not *do* to leave your guests. 'Tis bad *ton.*" She peered closely at her brother. "Is something wrong?"

He shook his head. "No, I needed a breath of fresh air, that's all." He offered his arm to her even though he longed to leave the ball altogether. "Let's return inside."

"I pray that you will dance with all the lovely young ladies here tonight. They don't want anything more than to please you. They—"

Terence shut out her prattle and gazed around the brightly lit ballroom. There was Toby, his face dark with disappointment. Missing Miss Warwick, no doubt, even if the room was full of lovely young ladies who liked nothing better than to flirt with eligible greenhorns. Annabelle Rushton stood some distance away staring at Toby as if he were a snake under a rock.

Terence sensed that someone was watching him, and he scanned the chairs along the wall. In a corner, his grandfather sat all alone. His old gaze burned across the stifling hot room, and Terence felt his heart constrict. His meeting with Miss Warwick had crushed his defenses, and the old man looked no more than a shrunken shadow of his old self. Mayhap McBorran didn't have long to live, like the old man had pointed out to Miss Warwick. Damn it all! That inveterate rake didn't deserve his forgiveness, not after stripping the entire family of its wealth *and* pride. Yet, guilt washed through Terence as he studied his grandfather surreptitiously. Even if McBorran had changed, how could all the pain he'd created in the past be wiped away? To his surprise, Terence realized that he didn't feel all that much pain. It was as if he was a different person than the angry, sullen man who had left for India ten years ago. The loss of a fortune was not as devastating as the loss of a mother. *I still blame McBorran for encouraging Mother to leave Scotland those many years ago. I have not forgiven him for that.* Terence felt the stab of the old pain, but somehow it wasn't as piercing as it once was. Had Miss Warwick filled some of the void? Had her quiet dignity started the healing of his heart? Confused, he shook his head. It was too momentous a question to contemplate.

Drusilla nudged his arm. "Go dance with your guests, Terence. It's high time you find a lady to wed. This house needs the patter of small feet."

Terence looked at his plump sister in surprise. It was the first time she'd ever ordered him to do anything in a forthright manner. Usually she took her handkerchief and her vapors into play.

"Tell me, Dru, how did you feel when Grandfather came to your door after so many years?"

Drusilla flapped her fan nervously. "I was taken aback, of course, but he is the head of the family whether we like it or not." She made clucking sounds with her tongue. "Strangely enough, he begged my forgiveness after all these years. Not that his actions much altered my life, but he brought a taint to the Farnsworth name." Drusilla's voice lowered to a whisper. "But so did our mother, even more."

Terence flinched as if slapped. Odd that Drusilla should bring up the subject uppermost in his mind. Did Mother's betrayal still affect her life?

"Did you give him your forgiveness?"

Drusilla shrugged. "I suppose we never were estranged. The situation didn't distress me as much as it did you."

Terence seethed with anger. "What consummate effrontery of the man to enter my house uninvited, especially at an event when I can't show him the door."

"Grandfather always was a devious man, but I feel that he's a different person than he was twenty years ago. He gets along famously with Toby."

"Toby is a young twiddlepoop. He does not have the

experience to cull the wheat from the chaff. His infatuation with Miss Warwick is an example of that."

Drusilla staggered against him and whipped her fan back and forth in agitation. "I'm so grateful that *person* did not attend. It was humiliating enough to smile at Miss Turnbull. It positively made my teeth ache." She sent a probing glance at her brother. "Tell me, Terence, have you paid off that hussy? Toby has spent more time at home, moping about. I hoped it might be from a broken heart."

Terence looked at her puffy face, noticing the hope in her eyes. Only a few weeks ago he would have been elated to see Toby separated from Miss Warwick, but then he'd truly believed that she was a strumpet. Now he wasn't at all sure. No, he suspected that he'd judged her wrongly from the start. He sucked in his breath as he realized that she'd convinced him more deeply of her innocence than he was comfortable with. She'd touched a part of him he didn't know existed.

"Don't worry, Dru, I have the situation under control. Toby shall not marry Miss Warwick."

Joanna was dozing on the sofa in the parlor when Aunt Oddy returned from the ball with Lord McBorran. The older woman laughed in elation at something McBorran muttered in her ear.

At that moment, Aunt Oddy noticed that they were not alone in the room. "Joanna! What in the world are you doing here in the darkness? Why aren't you sleeping in your bed?"

"I was waiting for you, but I could not stay awake." Joanna yawned, her head heavy from all the conflicting thoughts still rioting in her mind. "Did you enjoy the ball, Auntie?"

"Ohhh, Joanna you should have been there. I can't remember a more romantic evening. The ballroom was glittering splendor, the chandeliers ablaze with candlelight. The walls had cream brocade panels, and I've never seen so much gilt molding in my life. It was like entering a royal palace. And flowers! There were roses *everywhere*. The viscount had not spared any expense. The buffet was delicious: lobster patties, salmon rolled in bacon, trout in aspic, jellies, cakes, and strawberry tarts."

She sat down on the sofa, and the earl walked stiffly to one of the chairs. He had dark smudges under his eyes, and his face looked pale and drawn. Joanna got up and emptied the last of the brandy on the sideboard into a snifter. She gave it to the old man. "Tell me, Lord McBorran, did you have a chance to speak with Lord Perth?"

"Aye, six words," he said in a voice laced with disappointment. "Good evening, thank you, and good night. He would not acknowledge me at all."

Joanna sat back down. "Oh, how wretched. I'm sorry. You should have insisted on speaking with him."

The earl waved his hand carelessly, but Joanna sensed his despair. "There will be other times. I wanted him to see me, to get the idea that we're still family, whether he likes it or not."

"You'll see that he'll come around in the end, even though he is a stiff-rumped fool." Joanna clapped her hand to her mouth as the words slipped out. "I shouldn't have said—"

The earl leaned back in the chair and laughed. "Terence is that, and more. But he's had many trials in the past. One can't but understand his reluctance to see me, or anyone who reminds him of his past."

Joanna felt a strange need to know more. She was soaking in every minute detail about her neighbor, and she feared it wasn't due to barefaced curiosity, but to a deeper need.

As she was about to open her mouth, a knock sounded on the front door.

"By Jupiter, who is visiting at this late hour of the night?" Lord McBorran wondered aloud. He began to rise, but Joanna waved him down.

"Don't bestir yourself. I'll find out who it is."

The pounding continued, and Joanna pressed her ear to the door. "Who is it?"

"Toby. Joanna, open up. I saw the lights on in the house. Is something wrong?" He sounded genuinely concerned, and Joanna unlocked the door.

"Toby? Why aren't you at home at this ungodly hour?"

He came in, looking handsome in his formal evening wear. But Joanna deduced by his scowl that the ball had squashed his youthful high spirits.

"I was disappointed that you did not attend the ball. Uncle Terence said you'd accepted the invitation."

"Your great-grandfather is here," Joanna said, evading the question. "He brought Miss Turnbull home."

Toby brightened at the mention of Lord McBorran. " 'Pon rep, old Angus here?" He stepped into the parlor after divesting himself of hat and cloak in the hallway. He bowed to Aunt Oddy and shook hands with his great-grandfather.

"It took a lot of gumption to beard Terence in his den," he said to McBorran and slapped his back. "My uncle looked flushed and tight of lip, and I feared he would tip you a settler." Toby laughed. "That would have been a proper set-to."

"Terence is much too concerned with propriety to create a scene at his own ball. Anyone could guess that." McBorran sipped his brandy, and his eyes twinkled over the rim. "But I must admit I was curious to see his reaction. I thought he might cut up rough, but he greeted me in an icy, most civil voice. After that, he ignored me completely." The old man sighed and poked the tip of his cane at Toby's leg. "And you, young blighter, why did you wander about with a long face?

There were any number of debutantes who would have swooned at one of your smiles." He gave Joanna a wink. "I take it the right lady was not there."

Toby gave an impatient snort. "I only spoke with Annabelle Rushton briefly, and only that because Uncle Terence forced me to dance with her. She has two left feet, and that's all there is to it."

"A dead bore, hey? I thought you made a handsome couple," the earl went on. "Mighty handsome."

Toby gave Joanna a soul-searing glance. "Miss Rushton holds no candle to the woman I—"

"Toby, do you want a cup of tea?" Joanna asked before he could utter the damaging words. She was getting thoroughly annoyed with Toby's love-struck expression. He only shook his head and glanced to the floor.

"I don't know what's wrong with the young moonlings today. 'Tis clear to me that Miss Rushton is mightily taken with you, Toby," said Aunt Oddy. "She blushed brighter than a lantern when she clapped eyes on you. I've always come to the conclusion that there's unfinished business between the two of you."

Toby straightened, a mutinous look on his face. "Miss Rushton and I have nothing in common except old memories, and that's the end of it."

Silence fell in the room, and Joanna hid a yawn behind her hand. It had been a long, emotionally draining day. She didn't know what to think of Lord Perth and his family anymore. What she needed was a good night's rest.

Toby came to stand beside her as Aunt Oddy immersed the earl in conversation about the evening's entertainment.

"Is there a problem, Toby?" Joanna asked.

He seemed to debate what to tell her. "Well . . . I heard some gossip tonight. It appears that Leslie Frinton is about to get leg-shackled, to a damsel in

Devonshire." Toby pursed his lips in thought. "I wonder if she's aware of the scandal he created in London."

Joanna could not suppress a feeling of gratitude toward the young man. Ever since the first day they'd met, he'd been willing to put all the blame for her disgrace on Leslie Frinton. "I know nothing about it."

"The man should be drawn and quartered for what he did to you, Joanna. In fact, I think I shall make a trip west and confront the fellow, or send someone."

"Oh no! You will gain nothing from haring off to Devon. Frinton will never admit that he was wrong."

"I would want nothing more than to see your name cleared, Joanna."

Joanna touched his hand in appreciation. "You're the best friend a person would want," she said with a smile.

"Friendship is not what I want," he said stiffly. He rose and bowed to the company. He pressed a fervent kiss to Joanna's fingers. "I will be back."

Thirteen

The following Saturday Joanna and Aunt Oddy traveled five miles west to the market in Alfriston. Since it was located on a river and close to the coast, the town had been, and perhaps still was, a popular smugglers' spot. Half-timbered buildings with latticed windows lined the high street, one of them, the notorious tavern The Star.

Joanna was anxious to view the display of her madonna lilies and peonies at Hobson's stall. The flowers were early bloomers due to the unseasonable heat, and the coins that Hobson had given her for them—besides a bag of wheat flour—jingled in her reticule. She would buy a birthday present for Aunt Oddy, perhaps a new straw bonnet with a wide blue ribbon if she could find one. Blue was Aunt Oddy's favorite color.

As they left Daisy and the gig at the livery stables, Aunt Oddy said, "Look, there's Miss Rushton and her mother. Let's pay our respects."

"I don't know . . ." Reluctantly, Joanna followed her plump aunt, who bustled across the inn yard and greeted the Rushtons. Annabelle's mother gave Joanna a cautious glance and acknowledged her with a curt nod. Joanna inhaled sharply, feeling the wave of panic that always filled her when she encountered any member of the local gentry. At least Mrs. Rushton wasn't as rude as some.

Annabelle sidled away from her parent and spoke to Joanna in an undertone. "I missed you at Lord Perth's ball. I barely knew anyone present, and it was most embarrassing. As you know, Mother and I mostly keep to ourselves. Oh Joanna, it was as dull as ditch water."

Joanna smiled. "It couldn't have been that horrid. You must have danced with any number of young gentlemen."

Annabelle heaved a profound sigh. "Greenhorns the lot, pimply and tongue-tied. I've never been so bored."

"You're most exacting, Annabelle, but I suppose the balls in London are a lot more dashing than our country dos. Still, Oddy told me that the viscount only served the finest of everything." Joanna glanced at the younger woman's frowning face. "Not to your taste? Really, some part of the festivities must have caught your interest. Toby told me he danced with you."

Annabelle snorted. "That lummox! I swear he has two left feet."

Joanna stifled a ripple of laughter. She couldn't very well disclose that Toby had said the same of Annabelle. She swallowed twice to make sure her voice was level before she spoke. "I'm sure he's not as bad a dancer as all that. I think Toby is a very attractive young man."

Annabelle's face darkened with disgust. "He has eyes for no one but himself and—you."

Joanna hid her mouth behind her hand, but she knew she could not conceal the twinkle in her eye. "Does it upset you greatly that he's taken with an *older* lady?"

Annabelle looked away quickly and chewed briefly on her bottom lip. "Of course not! How can you ask such a wretched question?"

Joanna fiddled with her reticule and said casually, "I had the impression that you care more for Toby than you're willing to admit."

The redness in Annabelle's cheeks expressed her agitation. "I don't know what gave you that idea. For as long as I can remember, I played with Toby during the summers. We were childhood friends. But when we grew up . . . well, it was different. Why would I be so narrow-minded as to care where Toby bestows his affection?"

Joanna stared at the line of wagons and drays that brought goods from the farms to sell at market. Pigs squealed in a pen, and prospective customers inspected a line of horses. "You must have liked him when you were children. Otherwise you would not have played together. And perhaps those feelings remain."

"Yes . . . we liked each other well enough. Toby enjoys riding just as much as I do, but that doesn't signify—"

"Well then, what happened to ruin your friendship?" Joanna asked inexorably. She wanted to get to the bottom of the problem. She observed Annabelle's face and noticed the various emotions dancing across her features: fear, hope, longing, and chagrin.

"You can tell me, Annabelle."

The young woman's eyes held a stormy expression. "So that you can disclose my woes to Toby?"

"Not at all! I don't tattle on my friends, and we are friends, are we not?"

"Of course we are!" Annabelle threw a glance at her mother, who was still in conversation with Aunt Oddy. She pulled the sleeve of Joanna's faded rose spencer and urged her aside. "You have to promise not to breathe a word to anyone—least of all Toby—that I spoke with you."

"Hand upon my heart, I promise."

Annabelle sat down on a barrel, uncaring if she soiled her threadbare muslin gown. "Before Toby went off to university, we—well, he asked me if I would wait for him, if we could get engaged before he left."

"Did you agree?"

Annabelle nodded, her neck bowed in misery. "I was very young and flighty, and still am in many ways. Six months after Toby left, I lost my heart to another fellow. He had the title of earl, no less, and Toby accused me of jilting him for a title and a fortune." She threw a desperate glance at Joanna. "The young earl was Harry Wishbourne. You know him, don't you? Mad about horses."

"He was not part of my circle in London."

Annabelle fished a handkerchief from her frayed brocade reticule and dabbed at her eyes. "Harry is forever kicking up a lark, and I doubt he'll ever grow up. I was torn in my feelings, but decided we wouldn't suit. Finally I gave him my congé. Toby called me a flighty piece who was born to ruin gentlemen's lives." She hiccuped discreetly and swallowed a sob. "He wouldn't forgive me."

"I think you did the right thing, Annabelle. Better that you saw the mistake before you tied yourself to a man you didn't love."

"I don't believe Harry cared one whit about me."

"I don't understand why Toby would ring a peal over your head for jilting Harry Wishbourne. It could be that he's still carrying the torch for you and is too proud to declare himself."

"Fiddle! Toby abhors me. He thinks I was horridly cruel to jilt two suitors in a row."

"It proves to me that he still cares deeply about you. Why else would he fly into a pet every time he sees you? He wouldn't if he didn't care."

Annabelle's face brightened, her tears glittering and her nose as red as a cherry. "You really think so?"

Joanna smiled ruefully. "And you? Do you reciprocate his feelings?"

"I . . . *think* I do. He's not the pimply youth I remember. During his time at Oxford, he became a gentleman—even though he has no manners whatsoever." She slid her gaze away. "I told him a few choice words myself, called him a ramshackle here-and-therian and a conceited fribble."

Joanna could not suppress her mirth. "A *fribble?*" She exploded, and several minutes passed before she could find her voice. "I would have liked to see his face at that moment. He rather fancies himself a sportsman and a country squire."

"My aim was to needle him where it hurt the most, in his vain heart. He vowed he would never speak to me again."

"No wonder Toby was furious," Joanna said when Annabelle had finished. "I think you ought to have a long talk with him and explain why you insulted him."

Annabelle wailed. "I've made such a muddle of things. You think he will listen to me? Understand?"

"Toby has a level head on his shoulders. I don't see why he wouldn't understand. After all, some years have passed since you parted, and he's bound to be more grown up. If anything, Toby is a gentleman."

Annabelle brightened. "I feel ever so much better after unburdening my heart."

Joanna laughed and squeezed Annabelle's thin hand. "That's what friends are for."

Annabelle grew pensive once more. "There is one thing that bothers me. Mother discovered that Lord Perth has no intention whatsoever of courting me. Now she wants me to marry one of Father's old acquaintances, Major Stone. She says I need a steadying hand and a secure future. Why, the fossil is old enough to be my father."

Joanna was going to pry into the matter more closely, but Aunt Oddy was beckoning her.

Mrs. Rushton called to her daughter, and the young woman grimaced. "I wish I could stroll with you, Joanna, but I know what Mother would say." She pulled her eyebrows together in a severe frown and imitated her parent's pinched voice, " 'Tis not seemly, Belle. We must keep ourselves to ourselves and cause no trouble."

Joanna smiled. "In this case, you must obey your mother."

Joanna parted from her friend and linked her arm with Aunt Oddy's. They strolled among the stalls that carried everything from spices and fruit to kitchen utensils and sewing implements. Joanna dawdled at a stall filled with ribbons and lace-edged handkerchiefs. Her earnings would not cover any extravagant purchases, except Oddy's birthday present. Enticing scents emanated from a stall filled with pastries, and a faint aroma of ale hung over the area.

The day was sunny without a single threatening cloud on the horizon. An old man was cranking the handle of a hurdy-gurdy at the end of the row of stalls, the twangy music mixing with the shrieks of children. A black mongrel carried a hat around for alms, and Joanna chuckled as she donated a small coin. The canine flourished an elegant leg. "Why, you are a gallant dog! I wish I could teach our spoiled cats a trick or two," she added to Aunt Oddy.

"They have a mind of their own. Isn't it a lovely day to be abroad?" Oddy said with a sigh of pleasure. "I'm so glad we decided to make the trip to Alfriston. We mope about at home too much as it is."

"Yes, you're right, of course. 'Tis not fair that you should have to suffer my disgrace like a prison sentence. The confinement must chafe against your patience sorely."

"Oh, my needs are humble. As long as we have a roof over our heads, I will not complain. . . ." Her words petered out, and Joanna felt the by now familiar pressure of anguish in her chest. They were not starving, but they had few luxuries, no frills and furbelows.

Their gowns were slowly falling apart, and their shoes would not last another season.

Joanna wanted to soothe her aunt, but she could not find adequate words. She wondered where she would scrape together the funds to pay for Daisy's feed and the coal to heat the house in the winter. Any word of reassurance withered on her tongue, and quiet despair welled up in her.

"Why don't you go and purchase the sewing thread you need, Auntie? We shall meet here in half an hour."

Oddy smiled and winked slyly. "Do you have a secret appointment with someone—a gentleman, perhaps?"

Joanna straightened her back decisively. "Don't be a ninny, Aunt Oddy. You know I don't." She turned on her heel before her aunt could say anything else, and walked back toward the stall that sold hats of all shapes. Chattering with the shop woman, she viewed the straw hats with wide brims, and others shaped as bonnets with a poke front. Such a bonnet would be like wearing blinders, she thought, and remembered that Aunt Oddy liked to look around herself with wide-eyed curiosity.

She held up the simplest hat she could find, and the saleswoman gave her the price: five shillings. Joanna set the hat down quickly, knowing that if she bought it, she would not be able to afford anything else. For a moment she felt close to tears, as if her straitened circumstances were too hard to bear.

The fat proprietress pulled out a stack of used straw hats from a wooden box behind the stall. "I 'ave these, a shillin' a piece. Ye could always add a new ribbon, melady."

Joanna looked at the hats with revulsion. They were soiled and dark with old perspiration. "No." Without letting her worry for the future rule her decision, she picked up the new hat and delved into her reticule for the coins. "I'll give you two shillings for this."

The shop woman rubbed her fingers and squinted at Joanna. "Four shillings, and not a groat less."

"Three, that's my last bid, and you'll give me a blue ribbon as well." Joanna jingled her coins in one hand.

The woman's eyes narrowed to slits. "Three and six, and I'll add th' finest ribbon to th' purchase."

"Done!" Joanna counted out the coins and received the folded ribbon, which she stuck into her reticule.

The crone wrapped the hat in coarse paper and tied a string around it upon Joanna's request. Feeling elated at her successful purchase, Joanna twirled the package in her hand as she walked along the stalls. While in an expansive mood, she bought a bag of sweets and popped one into her mouth.

Humming a song, she turned around and came eye to eye with Lord Perth, Mrs. Brownstoke, Toby, and behind the group, Premwar with Siddons on his shoulder. People stopped and stared at the turban-wearing foreigner and the monkey dressed in Perth livery, burgundy satin with gold braid.

"Miss Warwick," Lord Perth said with a smooth bow.

Joanna's heart lurched in her chest. She lost her speech as she gazed into his dark eyes, but she could read no indication that he remembered their meeting on the dock, let alone cherished the memory.

"Joanna!" Toby cried, and hurried to her side. He kissed her hand fervently, and Joanna pulled away. It disturbed her greatly to have the viscount witness Toby's amorous exuberance.

Lord Perth stared at her with an expression of interest, and at Toby's hand holding hers, with contempt.

"I'm so delighted to see you, Joanna. I didn't expect . . ." Toby's voice trailed off in embarrassment.

"I know. I'm the last person you expected to see in

public." She smiled primly. "But I'm not a prisoner at Newgate, nor am I a leper."

The viscount's lips lifted at the corners. "Well said, Miss Warwick, but what *are* you?"

"I didn't mean—I never thought—I should have—" Toby floundered. He squeezed her hand agitatedly.

"Don't act like a yokel, Toby," the viscount drawled, "and don't maul Miss Warwick's hand. You don't want to make her into a cripple." He gave her a sly look. "She needs her hands for gardening, and . . . other . . . activities."

"Toby!" Drusilla said shrilly as she reached her son. "Come here this instant! There's no need to linger. I'm completely at sea why we're in this town at all. It smells of horse's—er . . . ale, and brandy. You know I can't abide the smells of cattle and pig."

"Surely, Drusilla, a trip to the market can be quite . . . interesting. It all depends on who you meet." The viscount stroked his chin and gazed at Joanna through half-closed eyes. She felt prickly all over and heat rose to her cheeks.

Drusilla said, "Well, if it weren't for Lady Pemmerton, I certainly would not attend. She and her daughters would meet us here. Daphne is quite a catch, you know, Terence, and she told me that she would thoroughly enjoy seeing you again." She waved a scented handkerchief in front of her face. "I had no idea that it would be so obnoxiously odorous, and so filled with *creatures*." She fixed Joanna with a terrible eye.

"There might be a cockfight or two," Toby said hopefully. "Are those the creatures you mean, Mother? Nothing wrong with a fight, is there?"

Drusilla made a sound deep in her throat as if she was about to swoon. She fumbled for the support of Lord Perth's strong arm. "All that *blood*," she said faintly.

"I think your mother meant beasts of a more flighty nature," Joanna said with ice in her voice. "Birds of paradise, for instance."

Toby's mouth fell open, and Lord Perth's gaze sharpened.

"Joanna, my sweet! You're not supposed to know about such—individuals," Toby blurted out, aghast.

Joanna felt reckless. She stiffened her back and lifted her chin. "Surely everyone knows what those birds are, even your mother."

Drusilla swayed dangerously, and Joanna could not stifle a gurgle of laughter. Lord Perth's presence compelled her to look at him, and she noted the amused twinkle in his eyes. Otherwise, his face remained expressionless.

A flame, strong and happy, sprang to life in her chest and filled her blood with bubbles that made her lightheaded. The world receded for a moment, and there was only Lord Perth's face and his intense dark gaze. It touched her all the way to her toes, and she felt her blush deepening. He'd touched her without reaching out; he'd spoken without saying a single word. But what did it all mean to her? More danger? Another chapter in his nefarious game? Or had he really come to care for her? *Balderdash!* she chided silently. *Don't be a goose, Joanna. He's only trying to take advantage of you, find your weak spots and deal you a death blow through one of those.*

Drusilla said hoarsely, "I feel sadly out of curl, Terence. I demand that you take me back to the carriage. We must leave *this instant*. It won't do to mingle with the rabble too long, or their bad manners might rub off on us."

"But we just arrived," Terence said mildly. "The best is yet to come."

"What, the cockfight?" Joanna asked innocently. "Or have you entered Siddons in a thieving contest?"

The viscount barked a laugh. "I think she would win any contest; she has already gathered a large crowd."

Joanna noticed the farmers and children discussing the monkey as it sat on Premwar's shoulder. The baker passed with a tray of raisin buns on his shoulder, and Siddons snaked out her hairy arm and stole a bun. She screeched in excitement, but the baker proceeded without noticing anything amiss. The crowd laughed uproariously.

"She would certainly win any contest of bun snatching," Joanna said dryly. "She'll be reported to the constable."

"Are you going to do it?" the viscount asked in a low voice. "To save everyone else the trouble. It would be so like you to ruin the day."

"I suspect any such act on my part would send you into high fidgets, milord. I'm not sure I dare to provoke you in such a way."

He leaned closer to her ear. "Everything you do provokes me—in many ways."

"Dang me if that dog didn't flourish a bow!" cried Toby as he spied the dog passing the hat. "I've never seen anything so barmy in all my life."

"Language, Toby. My head is spinning horribly from all the verbal abuse I've had to take this morning," Drusilla lamented, and took her handkerchief into play. She clutched Toby's arm feebly. "Please take me away from this dreadful place. I shall succumb to a fit of the vapors presently if you don't save me."

Toby sent Joanna a look of despair, but she waved him on. "Come to tea, Toby. I want to show you my latest additions in the garden."

He brightened. "I shall count the minutes till I see you again."

Siddons jumped onto the viscount's shoulder and dripped crumbs all over his tailored coat of blue superfine. Joanna saw details she hadn't really noticed before: the hard angle of his jaw that spoke of strength, the streaks of red in his hair that the sunlight enhanced, the fine web of lines at the corners of his eyes. The flash of brilliance in his eyes. Every part helped to attract her attention, and every time she encountered Lord Perth, he seemed to grow in magnificence. All she'd ever experienced before in his presence was her own momentous anger, except during that last encounter on the dock.

He offered his arm. "Would you give Siddons and me the pleasure of strolling the length of the stalls?"

She hesitated. "So that you can give me another set-down? I'm not sure I'm willing to ruin this perfectly splendid day."

"I shall curb my acid tongue for the moment."

She placed her hand in the crook of his elbow, and a jolt of pleasure spread through her. This was not how she ought to react to her enemy!

They stopped at the baker's stall and the viscount paid for the bun that Siddons had stolen. "It won't do to end up in the roundhouse for a crime perpetrated by my monkey. The turnkey would never stop laughing."

Joanna tried to suppress her mirth. It wouldn't do to let the viscount think that she'd fallen for his roguish charm. It was much easier to dislike the other side of him, the stern censurer.

"When I was a boy," he said as they continued walking, "market day used to be my greatest pleasure. We weren't supposed to attend, but we always managed to sneak away from our tutor."

"We?" Joanna was acutely aware of the pressure of his arm, and she wondered if he felt the same about her.

"My cousin Jamie. He was always ready for a lark, and I wasn't far behind. Between us, we raided the larder and chased the piglets in their pen at McBorran Castle. We were severely scolded by my father, but that was before—" He went abruptly silent, and Joanna sensed a somber mood coming upon him.

"Is your father still alive?" She'd heard he wasn't, but she deemed it only polite to ask.

"No . . . he died many years ago, from a—" The viscount coughed as if she'd caught him in a compromising position. A flush had crept above the starched shirt points and into his cheeks. "I don't want to bore you with the story of my sad past, Miss Warwick." He directed her around a man pushing a hand cart. "Come, let's take—"

"You never bore me, Lord Perth," she responded truthfully.

He slanted a glance at her and smiled ruefully. "Nor do you make me yawn. Mayhap arguing makes life livelier."

"I don't argue as a rule, you know," Joanna said with some asperity. She looked at the locals clustered around the stalls. "You will get a bad reputation for spending so much time in my company, milord. They will say I'm leading you down a path of sin."

"I'm not a callow youth. 'Tis *you* who should not wander about on a gentleman's arm unchaperoned, Miss Warwick."

"Then you're the one who is leading me into sin." Joanna sighed as he smiled into her face. "But I don't care what they say about me anymore. They can whisper that I've set my cap on you, but we know the truth. That's all that matters to me."

He stopped and gazed deeply into her eyes. "Would it be so bad if you set your cap on me and not on Toby?"

She blushed and tore away from him. "Really! This is the outside of enough, Lord Perth. You have no right—I will not allow any more teasing remarks from you."

He followed her out on the meadow behind the stalls.

"I wasn't chiding you. I never realized that you've grown so bitter that you believe everything I say holds a hidden barb."

"I'm not bitter, only sensible." She stood with her back toward him while pretending to admire a clump of bluebells among the swaying timothy at her feet. "And you don't have to protect Toby by offering for me."

He made a sound that was something between a moan and a laugh. "You sound both bitter and defensive."

"And why shouldn't I be? No need to mock me about it." Joanna felt tears choking her throat. "You like to wound me, Lord Perth, because *you* are disillusioned."

Silence sagged heavily between them, and Joanna was acutely aware of each and every sound coming from the market. She pressed her knuckles to her mouth to stop herself from crying. Gulping down her tears, she stared dry-eyed at the horizon, and continued, "You have everything, milord. You have home and fortune, you have family, you even have a monkey who likes you. You have everything to be grateful about."

"I didn't always. I've worked for all I have. Not like my ancestors who had everything given to them."

When Siddons heard the word monkey, she jumped onto Joanna's shoulders and chattered in her ear. Joanna pulled her hand along the silky tail, and looked into Siddons's bright eyes. Breadcrumbs stuck to the leathery wrinkles around the monkey's mouth, and Joanna wiped them off.

"Hard toil forms the character they say. Tell me more," she added, not daring to face him.

He heaved a deep sigh and took her elbow. Together they walked toward the fence around one of the paddocks. Leaning against it, they viewed the horses trotting about and swishing their tails.

"Miss Warwick, you already know about Grandfather's spendthrift ways. He cared about no one but himself. He was a regular shabster, and I doubt that he's changed much despite his claim that he's a different person." He braced his elbows on the top rail and hung his head.

Joanna felt an unbidden flare of compassion. "Some gentlemen never shoulder the yoke of responsibility, as you so readily did. But at least you can speak to him once, let him explain. For once, forget your wounded pride."

The viscount slanted her a keen glance. "Why should I be so generous to someone who ruined my life?"

Joanna gave an unladylike snort. "He didn't ruin you, milord! Look at yourself, at the height of your power and confidence. Surely you would not have gathered such strength if everything had been given to you from the start. Adversity made you act, create your own life and fortune."

"You are very wise, Miss Warwick, but as annoying as a burr under my skin. Why should I listen to you?" He pushed his fists against the fence, and Joanna sensed his warring emotions. She scratched the monkey's chin.

"Yes, why should you listen to me? After all, I'm only a feeble-minded woman, and the pariah of polite society to boot."

His breath exploded out of his mouth. "Why do you have to remind me of that every time we meet?"

"We wouldn't meet if it weren't for your efforts to save Toby from my wicked schemes." Joanna's heart constricted at the truth of those words. She swallowed her pain as she realized that she could no longer keep up the pretense that she would marry Toby. Deeply tired, she said, "But don't worry, I won't harm Toby in any way."

His face brightened, and his eyes gleamed with appreciation. "Does that mean you're willing to let him go?"

Joanna nodded. "For the benefit of neighborly peace, I have retracted my clinging claws." The truth was that she'd never enticed Toby into her house, nor had she cajoled his affection. But she was not about to explain the truth to the viscount.

He caught her hand in his, and she felt the warmth of his touch coursing up her arm. "I see that I've judged you unfairly, Miss Warwick. Mayhap there is more than a conniving heart behind your glorious blue eyes."

"Mayhap there is," Joanna said in a chiding voice. "You should have known that by now after our many . . . *encounters*. But 'tis said that gentlemen are blind." *Curse him,* she added silently. He'd thought nothing of their heated kisses that had rocked the foundation of her world. She continued, "Since you've eagerly solicited the promise that I relinquish my hold on Toby, and have received it, I suppose our dealings are now over." She lifted the monkey into his arms and turned abruptly away from him.

"Good day, Lord Perth. Enjoy your victory."

"Wait! We are far from finished—I need to speak with you about—about—*us*."

She hurried across the grass. "You got what you wanted all along. I have nothing else to say to you."

Fourteen

"Lord Perth is unscrupulous and hard. He cares only about the precious reputation of his family," Joanna said in disgust. She wound her arm through Aunt Oddy's as they walked toward the gig. After her meeting with Lord Perth, Joanna wanted nothing more than to return home. "He's cruel and cold, boorish, and full of pride."

"I've never seen you so overset, Jo. Whatever happened to bring on this verbal tide of vinegar?" Aunt Oddy patted her niece's arm. "Did Lord Perth act in an ungentlemanly fashion toward you?"

"He didn't *act* in any particular way, Auntie, but that does not mean he's a gentleman. If he were, he would not have taken for granted that I was a fallen woman intent on Toby's ruination."

Aunt Oddy fanned herself and breathed deeply in agitation. "Dear me, that might be true, but most people would accept the general censure of your reputation without question. Surely the viscount is no different."

"He could have given me the benefit of the doubt, Auntie. He could have!"

"Heavens, I never realized there was such depth of vitriol between you and our neighbor."

"He's a high-handed bore and a misogynist." Joanna tossed their purchases into the gig and grabbed the reins as if they were her only lifeline. Striving to suppress the tight ache in her chest, she helped her aunt into the carriage. It hurt more than she'd thought possible that the viscount cared naught for her feelings.

Aunt Oddy settled her gown around her on the seat and made sure the lace fichu lay straight over her ample bosom. "The viscount has had many disappointments in his life, dissolutions that surely ruined his faith in goodness. But you can't hold that against him, Jo. He's a bitter man, not angry at you in particular."

Joanna bit down hard on her bottom lip. "He had no right to pretend his . . . his appreciation of me." She flicked the reins over Daisy's sagging back. "I've been such a gullible fool."

Aunt Oddy fluttered her hands helplessly. "His *appreciation*? My dear, I must confess I haven't the faintest notion what you're on about."

"I'll never forgive myself for being bamboozled by that scoundrel." Joanna fell silent as she turned their equipage homeward.

Aunt Oddy sat stiffly beside her as if deep in thought. As they left the sounds and smells of the market behind, she said, "Jo, are you trying to tell me that you are enamored with—Lord Perth?" She turned her round eyes upon her niece, and Joanna stifled a nervous laugh.

"I suppose there's no use denying that I've been daft enough to cultivate a *tendre* for that odious man."

"Don't flay yourself, Jo, for wearing your heart upon your sleeve."

"I've acted like a veritable goosecap! I've never felt more foolish in my life." Joanna gazed at the hedges lining the lane and wondered if she should go to ground like a badger and only come out to forage at night.

"Mayhap the viscount will offer for you," Oddy said without much conviction.

"Ha! And the moon is made of cheese. He would not

sully his reputation by marrying a 'fallen' woman." She pulled at the left rein to urge Daisy to step aside for an approaching carriage.

Aunt Oddy fanned her face. "There is that, of course. Oh, I wish I could wring that miserable Leslie Frinton's neck. He ruined your life. 'Tis not fair!"

The approaching carriage came to a halt beside them and Joanna pulled Daisy to a stop when she recognized Lord Thistlethorpe's brougham. He leaned out the window, the wooden frame threatening to flatten his cresting hair arrangement.

"Miss Warwick, Miss Turnbull! If only I'd known you would venture into Alfriston, I'd offered you seats in my coach."

"Thank you kindly," Aunt Oddy said politely. "But we're making the return journey after concluding our purchases."

Joanna shuddered as she met his calculating gaze. He clutched the frame, and she noticed that rings of all shapes adorned every finger except the thumbs. She also noticed the dark rims under his long fingernails, and the thought of those hands on any part of her anatomy made her cringe.

"My dear Miss Warwick—Joanna, I expected you to stay at home pondering our last conversation. I'm surprised to meet you in public, during your—indubitably—frivolous mission to the market."

"Frivolous, milord? I'm not a leper who has to hide away from civilization," Joanna said sharply, and Aunt Oddy nudged her in the side lest she say something that would provoke the old lecher's wrath.

"There's only one day left until the time is up, Joanna. I've been uncommonly patient, but now I am counting the hours till you be mine."

Never! Joanna thought. A clatter of hooves and the rattle of wheels approached from behind. She was relieved that the meeting would be cut short. She glanced over her shoulder and recognized Lord Perth atop a handsome gray stallion, and the crested Perth coach farther behind.

She fought down the urge to whip Daisy into a gallop. Nothing could be accomplished by rash actions, which Daisy was well aware of. *Besides, I have no whip,* Joanna thought.

"Ah! There you are, Miss Warwick," the viscount called out, worry evident in every line of his face. "You left rather abruptly. Escape, I would call it."

"There was no reason for me to linger," she said. She lowered her gaze. He had reined in right behind the gig, and she could feel him studying her closely.

"Did you visit the market on Perth's invitation?" Thistlethorpe asked, his voice laced with suspicion.

Loath to have to explain herself, Joanna nevertheless said, "No, Lord Perth's party happened to arrive after we did. Mrs. Brownstoke and her son are in the carriage." She flicked the reins to urge the mare forward. "We can't stop in the middle of the road like this. We're certain to create an accident. Good afternoon, Lord Thistlethorpe."

"I expect you to give me an answer, Joanna. I will give you two more days, not a minute longer," he called after them. "I shall present myself at your house at precisely eleven o'clock on Monday morning."

Joanna flinched as a cold wave of apprehension washed over her. "I shall keep my promise," she cried, but added in a whisper, "to myself." *A pox on all gentlemen!* Especially the two lords, Thistlethorpe and Perth.

The viscount listened to Thistlethorpe's demand and wondered what kind of answer the old roué expected from Joanna Warwick. There could only be one, a response to a marital offer. The thought of Joanna marrying that slimy toad made Terence's blood boil. As he watched Daisy putting more distance between himself and the intriguing Joanna Warwick, he realized that Joanna had touched him more deeply than he cared to admit. It was clear, however, that she cared naught for him. He'd opened his heart to her and divulged his anger and pain. For that he'd only gotten scorn in return. He'd never shown his frustrations to anyone until he met her. The novelty made him feel vulnerable as if Joanna had claimed some power over him.

Still, he'd gotten what he wanted. She'd promised to relinquish her hold on Toby. With a triumphant smile that didn't ease the ache in his heart, Terence urged his stallion forward.

Toby arrived in time for tea and Joanna greeted him in the garden. He helped to carry out the tray with the tea things and set it on the table under the wide-spreading oak tree. As usual, he viewed with great interest the mountain of scones that Mrs. Dibble had made. Since it was Aunt Oddy's birthday, Joanna had baked a cake for the occasion, but it was still in the larder. Mrs. Dibble would carry it outside in time for the second cup of tea.

Joanna had attached the blue ribbon to the straw hat and rewrapped it. She had smuggled the gift under the table, and it lay concealed by the long tablecloth beside Toby's rectangular package. Joanna thought her young admirer had been sweet to bring a present. Not everyone was as thoughtful and perceptive—Lord Perth came instantly to mind. Joanna frowned and pushed aside the thought. She arranged the silverware on the saucers and folded the napkins.

"I sent a note to Annabelle when we returned from market and invited her to tea. I hope you won't fly into a pet over it, Toby."

He opened and closed his mouth several times, and anger furrowed his brow. " 'Tis none of my business whom you invite to tea, but you know I can't abide that . . . *minx*. She's a thorn in my flesh."

Joanna rearranged the flowers in the vase at the center of the table. She slanted a glance at Toby and said, "Don't call her that. She's a singularly fine young woman." Joanna realized that if she broke her promise of silence to Annabelle, she might nudge Toby into forgiving her young friend. "As a matter of fact, I spoke with her this morning at the market."

She heard Toby cursing under his breath. He looked like he would slam his fists into the table, but instead he shoved them into his pockets. "What did she have to say? Did she speak ill about me? Probably all lies."

"I'm certain she still has deep feelings for you, Toby. She made one mistake and you ought not hold that against her for the rest of your life. 'Tis time to forgive and forget."

Toby dashed his hand through his carefully arranged hair. "One mistake perhaps, but it ruined my life. I've never been more miserable than when she accepted Harry Wishbourne's suit. Why, the man is a bounder! A libertine with not the slightest sense of responsibility."

"Annabelle found that out before it was too late." Joanna adopted a lighter tone of voice. "She's not married, and she loves you. When are you going to get that into your thick head?"

Toby fell backwards into a chair. "She told you that? A rasper if I ever heard one."

Joanna pursed her lips. "Perhaps not in so many words, but I read between the lines."

Confusion warred with chagrin on Toby's face. "I'll lay you a pony that she bamboozled you."

Joanna laughed. "I don't accept bets. Anyway, I would lose. Annabelle did not lie." She glanced toward the house. "Think about what I said. Aunt Oddy is coming."

They waited for Annabelle another fifteen minutes, but when she didn't arrive, Joanna served the tea. Perhaps Annabelle had been too embarrassed after her disclosure at the market to attend.

Joanna prattled about the morning. Once in a while, she threw a glance at her unusually quiet admirer. His face was set in a brown study. She suspected he wouldn't remain her admirer for much longer. Not if he had the least feeling left for Miss Rushton.

"Happy birthday, Aunt Oddy," Joanna cried as Mrs. Dibble finally brought out the fruit and almond cake adorned with ripples of whipped cream.

Oddy clapped her hand to her mouth. "Dear me! You remembered." She colored with pleasure and lowered her gaze. "I'm very touched."

Joanna nudged the still-dazed Toby, who bent to retrieve the packages. He gave Joanna hers to deliver into Oddy's hands.

Oddy reverently untied the string holding the paper together and beheld the straw hat with its dangling ribbon. " 'Tis just what I wanted, Jo. How did you know? Did you read my mind?"

Joanna smiled, savoring the warmth of giving in her heart. " 'Twas easy to see that your old one was crumbling more every day."

Aunt Oddy put on the hat over her frilly cap and tied the ends of the wide ribbon under her chin. She smiled hugely and patted Joanna's hand. "Thank you. I shall treasure it always."

Toby handed her his present, and she cooed over the book that was in under the wrapper. "*Guy Mannering,* by Sir Walter Scott. Ohhh, Toby, how did you know that I adore Sir Walter's writing?"

Toby shrugged, clearly embarrassed. "I noticed among the books in the parlor that you collect his works, Miss Turnbull. I heard his new book is all the rage in London."

Aunt Oddy clasped the volume to her bosom. "Oh, you thoughtful young man. Thank you."

The rest of the tea ritual was a lively event that ended with an empty scones' plate and a half-eaten cake. Aunt Oddy hastened inside to show Mrs. Dibble her gifts, and Joanna busied herself piling the dirty china onto the tray.

"Toby, have you thought about what I disclosed to you earlier?"

With a napkin, Toby wiped the crumbs off the plates for the sparrows on the ground. "Really, Joanna. I'm certain Annabelle slumguzzled you just to get my goat."

"I'm not an infant in leading strings who can be 'slumguzzled' at every turn. Annabelle did not lie to me."

He stared at her for a long moment, then put down the napkin. He took the tray from her and set it down. He lifted her hand and pressed it to his heart. His coat felt stiff against her fingers. "Joanna, 'tis you I . . . I love, not Annabelle Rushton. She's naught but an abominable little baggage."

Joanna gently withdrew her hand. "You are mayhap speaking in haste, Toby, without thought." She gazed into his adoring puppy eyes, but saw only the face of Lord Perth superimposed on the younger man's. They were startlingly alike in the shadow cast by the dense leaves.

Joanna could almost believe Toby's declaration of love, but she sensed this interlude was like a dream to him. One day he would wake up abruptly and realize he'd been afflicted with a bad case of infatuation.

She began to step away from him, but he gripped her arm as if in a fever. He pulled her jerkily toward him and embraced her. "I've longed to do this for a very long time," he said and, without further ado, planted his mouth on top of hers. He wound his arms tightly around her and pressed her close. His kiss was both passionate and clumsy. His sudden ardor made her push against him before the kiss could deepen. He finally lifted his head and stared into her face.

"It won't fadge, Toby!" she admonished when she could find her voice. "Let me go! Have you taken leave of your senses?" She stared into his dreamy eyes. "If you're set on acting like a cod's head, I order you out of my sight. This very moment."

He abruptly let go of her, a dazed look on his face. "Oh . . . dash it all! I'm terribly sorry for acting like a lout, Joanna. I was overcome by the scent of your violet perfume."

He blushed to the roots of his hair, and Joanna could not remain angry with him. Still, she remembered her promise to Lord Perth. She looked steadily at Toby and whispered, "I don't love you, Toby, and never will. I like you as a friend, but there can be no more than that. I'd rather you leave now. Our romance—or whatever it was—is finished."

Pain crossed his features and he opened his mouth to protest, but Joanna shook her head. "There's nothing else to say. One day you'll thank me for being honest with you."

He stared at her for a long moment, then turned on his heel and left. She heard him mutter to himself, "Toby, you damned maggot-witted wretch. You've ruined everything now."

Sounds of footsteps reached her ears, boots swishing against the ferns lining the path among the copper beeches. She knew who it was without turning around. Heaving a deep sigh, she brushed some crumbs from the tablecloth. "Good afternoon, Lord Perth. What brings you here?"

"Through the trees, I saw my nephew at your tea table. Mayhap I wanted to ascertain that you fulfilled your promise to turn Toby away," he said in an icy voice. "Instead, I witnessed a heated embrace. Really,

Miss Warwick, if you were a gentleman I would call you out."

Joanna kept her back toward him. "Spying is a paltry thing to do. Why didn't you step forward and announce your presence?"

"How could I interrupt such an intimate moment?" he asked scathingly.

"I'm sure consideration for the feelings of others is not at the top of your priorities."

"Nor is truthfulness one of yours." He took her arm and turned her around so that she had to face him. Wrath lay like a dark cloud over his features. "I was a fool to trust you and your promise that you would turn Toby away."

Joanna held her breath, feeling the explosion building inside her. If she opened her mouth, she would surely scream at him.

"I was taken in by your wiles, Miss Warwick, but believe you me, never again."

"You . . . *bacon brain!*" she flung at him. "You would not be able to read the truth if it was carved on a big sign right in front of your face. I've never met a more thick-skulled person in my life."

"Call me names, hurl insults at my face, but beware! You have trifled with me, and I don't take kindly to connivers like you."

"Go away! Plan your revenge. Roll me in pitch and string me up by my thumbs. I don't care for you, nor am I afraid of your threats." Joanna collected her scattered wits and lifted the tray. With a flurry of skirts, she stalked to the kitchen without a backwards glance.

Fifteen

Terence hesitated for a moment, feeling the sting of her scorn. Had he been wrong . . . had he—? He refused to finish the thought. His head filled with the red haze of fury at his inability to control his own life, the viscount returned home. He debated closing himself into his study with a bottle of brandy, but decided against it. Temporarily drowning his sorrows was not worth the headache in the morning. He went down the sloping lawn to the dock, gathered a handful of flat pebbles, and skipped each across the waves. One pebble touched the water ten times, and he was pleased. Fifteen minutes later, his ire had subsided to a smoldering glow. He sat down at the end of the dock and gazed out over the water, a satiny sheet of gold and blue that rippled softly as the breeze touched the lake. She had lied . . . cheated . . . fooled him. He'd been ready to believe everything she said once she'd worked her wiles on him. All his life, women had worked to undermine his life and equilibrium. Why did they have to go about business with lies and underhanded blows? They were no better than the pickpockets and charlatans in the streets. If you trusted one, she would invariably turn around and give you a punch in the solar plexus. God, he hated female machinations!

There must be some way to make Miss Warwick relinquish her hold on Toby. The viscount remembered Lord Thistlethorpe's cryptic words on the Alfriston road and decided to pay him a visit. Terence had a feeling that the older man knew something that might push Miss Warwick to the wall.

Or . . . could it be that he'd read her wrong, misunderstood her intentions? *No!* She'd fooled him somehow. He'd set out to seduce her and had instead become beguiled by her quiet air and lovely smile. He'd emptied his sorrow into her willing ears, and now she knew all his weaknesses. Some seducer he was! Some schemer she was.

Brushing off the tails of his coat and the seat of his inexpressibles, Terence went back up to the house. He noticed Toby sitting on the terrace, slouching in the shadows with a despondent air on his face. What had brought on that long face?

Terence joined his nephew on the wrought-iron bench and slapped his back. "Why so Friday-faced, Toby?"

Toby gave a wan smile and a desultory wave. "I've been pondering my life. In a few days, I'll come into my inheritance. I'll be truly considered a man for the first time, a man of substance. Why is it that I feel like a callow greenhead?"

Terence chuckled. "Believe you me, you'll feel that way periodically throughout life. Has someone put you in your place?" He immediately thought of Joanna, and wondered what she'd said to the young man before Toby left. Probably more promises and lies.

"No . . . I was only thinking. Tell me, Uncle, how would you best go about proposing to the lady that you love?"

Terence snorted. "I'm not the right man to ask, what with two rejections to my name. Why? I thought you already proposed to Miss Warwick any number of times. 'Tis bad *ton* to wear your heart in full view."

Toby gnawed on his knuckles. "I'm afraid I haven't shown much subtlety in my courtship. I've acted like a veritable imbecile."

Terence glanced at his nephew as suspicion filled him. "What? Has Miss Warwick cut you with the sharp side of her tongue?"

Toby shook his head vehemently. "Oh no, not at all!" He carried an unusual paleness of countenance. "She's a goddess, a kind, warm-hearted lady. 'Tis I who have comported myself like a complete flat."

Terence laughed coldly. " 'Pon rep, you only kissed her. I saw you. Don't get into high dudgeon, Toby. A woman like Miss Warwick thinks nothing of such a trifling faux pas. You did nothing that others haven't done before. A woman like—"

"Damn if you ain't a curst fellow!" Toby jolted to his feet and clenched his fists in front of his uncle's face. "If you as much as say one more derogatory word about Miss Joanna, I shall call you out. I mean it."

Terence pushed the threatening fists aside and took a deep breath to curb his temper. He could tell that Toby's patience had been sorely tried. He wished he knew what Miss Warwick had said to his nephew.

Toby gave him a dark look and sat back down. "You're a downy one, Uncle Terence, but Miss Joanna did not say anything to me that she didn't mean from the bottom of her heart. She's a thoroughly honest female—contrary to some others I know."

Terence bit back a howl of mirth. "Honest?" He longed to rant and rave about the depravity of Miss Warwick, but stopped himself in the nick of time. Any censure would surely fall to deaf ears. Toby was not the first young man to be taken in by a cunning female. Miss Warwick reminded him of his mother. The memory struck him like a hard blow in his chest, and however much he struggled to push it back into obscurity, it kept running through his mind like the rough side of a file. Could it be that he had to live through that humiliation again before he could exorcise the ghost of the deceitful Lady Perth? The lovely face of his mother swam before his vision, the soft brown hair and doe-like eyes that were deceptively innocent. That was before the ravishment of her beauty. Afterwards, she'd been as coarse and painted as a Covent Garden courtesan.

"I *said* honest. Are you going to give me a lecture on the feeble female brain?" Toby asked scathingly.

Terence bent a thoughtful eye on his nephew. Toby had grown up in these last few weeks, no longer treating his uncle with fawning admiration. "I don't think so. Like you pointed out, you are a grown man." He exhaled slowly. "And I would expect you to make the right choices, and not act like a moonling. . . ."

"That's what she said—that I acted like a regular cod's head." Toby continued chewing on his knuckles. "I have to find a way to correct an old wrong, Uncle. Miss Joanna told me most sharply."

Terence battled a surge of anger. "*What* did she demand? Money? I hope she didn't fill your mind with nonsense."

Evidently, Toby was not listening. "Miss Joanna is a most needle-witted female. Unlike me, she would not be afraid to confront old problems and set them right. I've been blind to the truth in my heart, and made a cake of myself at fair Joanna's feet."

"I'm sorry, old fellow, but I can't follow your reasoning."

Toby glanced up with a dazed look on his face. "No need to worry your head about me, Uncle. I'll come about, but I need to think—alone."

"A habit you're rather unaccustomed to, aren't you?" the viscount grumbled to deaf ears. Sighing, he stood. He said to himself as he left, "I suppose you were taught no more than drinking and wenching at Oxford. It cost me a pretty penny."

Terence rode through Hasselton Village in the late afternoon. The heat haze hung like a cloud of dust over the cottages lining the road. Chickens scratched in the hard-packed dirt, and giggling barefoot children ran after his horse. Terence was not in the mood to giggle with them. He was heading to Lord Thistlethorpe's dark mansion at the other end of the village.

Huge elms spread beside the long, winding drive. Grass grew among the gravel, and Terence realized it wouldn't be long before the estate took on an air of neglect. The old roué was probably too tight-fisted to spend anything on the upkeep of the lovely Elizabethan mansion. The red brick gleamed mellow in the sunlight, but Terence spotted several broken windowpanes. The maze hedges had not been clipped for a long time, and the rose bushes in the borders grew in scraggly disarray. Terence could not abide such lax maintenance; he liked everything tidy and cared for.

The butler admitted him and led him through the dim interior of the musty house to a library. Thistlethorpe sat in the gloom among his dusty and mildew-scented books and played solitaire with a battered deck of cards.

"Perth! I didn't expect to see you here," Thistlethorpe said in a peevish voice. "How can I assist you?" His bony fingers flashed over the cards, and Terence realized that gambling had been Thistlethorpe's true calling in life.

Perth came right to the point. "You're expecting some kind of answer from Miss Warwick. I overhead you telling her on the Alfriston road. I mean to know what you meant, and I'm not leaving until you tell me."

Thistlethorpe wiggled his eyebrows in a comical fashion. His eyes took on a sly cast. "Mere curiosity,

Perth, or is there something else prompting you to snoop? A *tendre* for the lady, mayhap?"

"Balderdash!" Unbidden, Terence sat down at the opposite side of the table covered with green baize. He wasn't going to reveal that he worried about Miss Warwick's safety. Why, he didn't even want to reveal to himself that he cared in the slightest about her well-being. "I might need something to settle a score with the . . . tart. Perhaps you can help me."

Thistlethorpe viewed him shrewdly from under bushy eyebrows. "I take violent dislike to your choice of words, Perth. What has she done to earn your scorn?"

"I'm afraid 'twould be most ungentlemanly to reveal any intimate details," Terence said, improvising. His eyes strayed to a sleeping moth-eaten cat on a pillow beside the old man, who petted it, and realized with a jolt that it was stuffed.

Thistlethorpe licked his lips. His hands sorted the cards seemingly without any pattern of thought.

"If you confide in me, I could make the deal handsomely profitable for you," Terence continued.

Thistlethorpe sneered. "I don't need your funds, impudent young puppy. What is it you think you'd get from me?"

Terence leaned across the table and bored his gaze into the older man. "The truth. What answer do you expect from Miss Warwick?"

Thistlethorpe pursed his lips and expelled a foul breath. Terence hurriedly leaned back in his chair. "What do you say, Thistlethorpe? What is it worth?"

"Well, I suppose 'tis no secret that Miss Warwick will presently become my wife. As you know, I'm very lonely in this mausoleum, especially at night without any female to warm my bones." He cackled and rubbed his hands in anticipation. "Miss Warwick has to accept my proposal by Monday. If she doesn't, she and her dotty aunt will find themselves expelled from Marsdon

Hall. Y'see, I lent her a goodly sum of money to pay off old Warwick's debts, with her house as collateral. Not that the hall is worth much, but I suspected she would have to marry me to protect herself from abject poverty. She's not been able to pay any of the monthly installments, and I won't accept getting nothing in return for my monetary outlay." He snorted. "You must see that I'm in my right to demand a settlement."

Loathing mixed with anger filled Terence's heart. He wouldn't wish his worst enemy to warm this lecher's old bones. Debauchery and ill health sat in every line of Thistlethorpe's face, and Terence wondered what kind of illness, or illnesses, the man had contracted during his wild days in the Metropolis.

"I'll pay you in full, plus interest, what Miss Warwick owes. You stand to make a handsome profit, which would enable you to purchase comfort for every night of the year."

"Hmmm, 'tis a tempting offer, but I've had my eyes on that particular young lady for quite some time. She's a choice morsel, and I can't wait to wind my arms around her."

The viscount saw his possibilities dwindling. "Take it from me, Thistlethorpe, Miss Warwick is a harpy. She won't give you anything but grief. In due time, she'll become a carping old horror. You'll be paying to get her off your hands."

Thistlethorpe chuckled. "You know how to bargain, young man. I suppose all those years in India taught you an astute business sense."

"That's correct, and I'm a stubborn man. I offer you triple interest."

Thistlethorpe rubbed his chin and peered closely at Terence, who wished he could read the older man's thoughts.

"I'd like to know why this is worth so much to you,

Perth. What does Miss Warwick possess that you need so badly?"

Toby's heart, Terence thought, but there was definitely a part of him that abhorred the thought of her, or anyone, falling into Thistlethorpe's clutches. Besides, he wasn't sure as to the true state of his own heart concerning Miss Warwick, but he didn't want to think about it. "You could always stake her debts in a gamble," he said casually. If Thistlethorpe was a true gambler, a bet might be irresistible to him.

Thistlethorpe rubbed his jaw, then caressed the stuffed feline at his side. "Hmmm, I don't know . . ."

Terence shuddered with revulsion. "I prefer chess, and I know you're a bruiser at all games. What do you say, Thistlethorpe? The first to win two games out of three."

Thistlethorpe slapped his hand onto the table. "Done! You're a man of my own heart. If you lose, you shall pay me the sum, plus interest, and I shall keep Miss Warwick's promissory note."

"Done!" Terence said, vowing that he would beat the old goat if it was the last thing he ever did.

The hours went by at snail's pace, Thistlethorpe pondering each step interminably. As darkness had fallen outside the dirty windows with their tatty drapes, the men shared a supper of cold cuts and four bottles of claret. Thistlethorpe drank most of the wine, and Terence kept filling the old man's glass. A clear head had the better chance of taking home the prize.

Avidly, Terence viewed the folded paper that stated that Miss Warwick owed Lord Thistlethorpe five thousand pounds. It would be in his pocket when he rode back home. He won the first game and thought the next one would be easy. It wasn't. Thistlethorpe out-foxed him, and he lost. The last game would be played from the edge of his seat. Terence wiped the palms of his hands on his thighs and took a deep breath. This game mattered more to him than any business deal he'd conducted in India. The realization annoyed him, but he set his mind on winning and went into the game with aplomb.

His stamina won out. The older man was sagging when, three hours later, Terence said, "Queen to King's Knight seven. Your king is trapped. Checkmate." Delirious with triumph and fatigue, Terence got up from the table and stretched his aching body. " 'Twas a hair-raising contest, but squarely won."

Thistlethorpe grumbled, but he seemed too tired and inebriated to dispute the victory. With a sneer, he pushed the promissory note across the table. "If anything can be said of me, 'tis that I'm not a sore loser. Here, take it."

With a smile, Terence folded the note and stuck it into his pocket. Soon enough, Miss Warwick would be forced out of Toby's world. This time, she would not be able to thwart him, Terence thought.

Sixteen

Toby paced the cramped parlor of the Rushtons' lodge in Hasselton. There were knickknacks on every surface, and he worried that he would push one of the figurines to the floor, or stumble on any of the numerous woven rugs. He clamped his arms to his back to prevent any straying cuff to act out of hand, and kept himself walking only back and forth on the long threadbare carpet of the vestibule. What was taking Mrs. Rushton so long? 'Twasn't like her to keep people kicking their heels as if they were servants of little value.

She came in, a pale pinch-faced stick of a woman, looking exactly as she had ten years ago. Toby remembered all his boyhood pranks in a rush and swallowed with mortification. Mrs. Rushton had a way of making him feel small and defenseless. She settled herself on a hard-backed chair and stared at him in a most disconcerting way. He swallowed hard and inserted a finger under his tight collar. He'd better plunge right into his proposal before he would lose his courage.

"Mrs. Rushton, as Captain Rushton is no longer with us, and there's no other male in the family, I turn to you for permission to marry your daughter Annabelle."

The lady swiveled her head, her expression stiff with surprise. "Really, Mr. Brownstoke? I'm not sure we understand each other correctly. These last few years you have not spoken to Annabelle. Why this sudden change of heart? I know that you had a falling out, and I'm certain that Annabelle holds you in very low esteem."

"Be that as it may, but I had to do the proper thing and approach you first in this matter. I'll explain to Annabelle if I get your permission—"

"Mr. Brownstoke! Not so fast. I thought you knew that another gentleman has expressed his interest in making Annabelle his wife. I've given him my consent."

Feeling as if the whole world had tilted on its axis, Toby paced the room. "Who is this gentleman?" he asked in a strangled voice. He flexed his hands, wishing he could punch the nincompoop who dared to desire his beloved.

"Major Stone. He was one of my husband's cronies."

Aghast, Toby stared at her set countenance. "Mrs. Rushton, you cannot possibly marry Annabelle to that bag of hot air! Why, he's old enough to be Annabelle's father, and a dead bore to boot."

Mrs. Rushton shrugged her bony shoulders. "Mr. Brownstoke, I take offense at your language! Major Stone is not a flighty young jackanapes like yourself. I'm sure Annabelle will be happy with someone who can curb her exuberance and hold her in a tight rein. I'm afraid my efforts to quell her hoydenish ways have been sadly unsuccessful."

"Quell her spirits!?" Toby tore at his hair in agitation. "You can't clip her wings like that. She'll be miserable."

Mrs. Rushton fixed him with a pale, unblinking stare. "What Annabelle needs most is a steadying hand and the creature comforts that are due to her."

Toby stopped in front of Annabelle's mother and held out his hands in a pleading gesture. "I can give her everything she needs. I'm not a skinflint like Major Stone.

I'll be twenty-one in a few days, and in the possession of a great fortune."

Mrs. Rushton eyed him frostily. "Major Stone will arrive in an hour to make his formal proposal to my daughter, and Annabelle will accept him. I'm sure of it."

"Please let me see her. Let me talk to her for five minutes alone, Mrs. Rushton. I assure you I will act in a wholly gentlemanly fashion."

Annabelle's mother rose, her mouth set into a stiff line. "Very well, let Annabelle tell you herself that she's not in the least interested in your offer."

Toby waited in frustrated agony as Mrs. Rushton went upstairs to inform her daughter that she had a visitor. What if Annabelle refused to see him? He would storm up the stairs and demand an interview. . . . Annabelle would have to see reason!

The door wrenched open and crashed against the wall. Like an avenging angel Annabelle stood on the threshold, her glorious eyes blazing and her wispy blond hair on end. "What are you doing here, Toby?"

"Dearest Annabelle, we need to discuss—"

"I have nothing to say that hasn't already been said. I've no interest in exchanging insults with you."

Toby marched up to her and gripped her hands in his. "Annabelle—sweetest—will you please listen to me? I've been an utter fool all these years, a veritable blockhead, a stubborn oaf, a low worm." He looked into her stormy eyes and longed to pull her into a tight embrace. "An insufferable idiot."

Annabelle's lips quivered, and tears brought brightness to her eyes. "You never forgave me."

"Before I went to Oxford, we pledged ourselves to each other, Annabelle. As soon as I was gone, you let the first fool that happened along turn your head." Toby tried to master his trembling tongue. "I was crushed."

"You forgot me as you went up to Oxford. I heard wild stories about you and your rakish friends."

"You can't hold that against me, Belle, I was devastated at your desertion."

They stared at each other for an interminable moment fraught with tension.

"We were greenhorns kicking up a lark," he continued lamely.

"You trifled with my feelings," she said in a small voice.

"You trifled with mine when you fell in love with Harry Wishbourne."

" 'Twas naught. My infatuation lasted a fortnight. You were so high in the instep that you wouldn't speak to me for three years." She slowly pulled her hands away. "I can't forgive you for that."

"Don't say that," Toby wailed, and fell down onto his knees. "Blister me, but I love you. I loved you then, and that's why I was so angry when you jilted me."

"I was lonely and miserable."

"You crushed my heart and I couldn't forgive you." He groaned and clutched one of her hands and covered it with kisses. "I'm older now, not so callow and foolish. Say that you forgive me."

She stared at him for a long time. "I don't know. I have to ponder—"

Toby clasped her hand to his heart. "Say that you'll marry me, Annabelle. I would be the happiest man in the world."

Her eyes grew round, and Toby sensed her shock. "Ma-marry you? But . . . but Mother has already decided that I shall wed Major Stone. His proposal to me is only a formality."

"You can't marry that prosy bore! He'll wake you up at dawn every morning with a trumpet blare and teach you to march. Is that what you want?"

Annabelle turned up her nose. "He likes equine sports as much as I do," she said with a sniff.

"Dearest Belle, listen to me—"

She looked away. "My ears burn with your drivel. Don't make such a cake of yourself, Toby, you look ridiculous on bent knees." She gave a sudden giggle. "Truly, I liked you better all sullen-eyed and stormy-tempered."

Toby's heart hardened. He got up and towered over her. Her thin face with its pointed chin held a mutinous look. He yearned to kiss the pouting mouth—and instantly acted on that wish. He gripped her elbows and pulled her into his embrace. Before she could protest, he'd covered her mouth with his. She tasted of honey and female sweetness, and he wondered why he hadn't had the rumgumption to do this before. His pride had hurt too much.

When he finally let go of her, he felt dazed in a very pleasurable way. "Tell me you accept my offer, sweetling."

She put her hands to her burning cheeks. "Oh dear, what am I to do? Maybe. I have to think." She pulled away from him. "You'd better leave now. I shall send you a note with my decision later today."

Toby fought an urge to plead with her. "I shall wait in agony at home until I get your answer," he said, and bowed formally.

Just before he left, she said, "I thought you had your mind set on marrying Miss Warwick. You've stuck like a burr to her side."

His cheeks grew hot. "Oh, *that*. Well, Joanna made me see the errors of my ways. She pointed out some painful truths about me, and I saw that she was right. To this moment I have acted like a blasted greenhorn. But no more. Joanna helped me realize my true feelings for you."

Annabelle's face brightened with a tender smile, and

Toby's heart constricted. As he gazed into his childhood friend's eyes he felt manly and protective, the latter feeling a wholly novel experience. "I shall pace my room until I hear from you." He clapped his beaver hat onto his head and left.

The note from Annabelle arrived late in the evening. By that time, he'd given up all hope. She had written in an agitated hand full of crossed-out words, and the paper was splotched with rain. Or was it tears? Holding his breath, he read the letter over and over.

> Dearest Toby,
>
> You must come at once to rescue me. I've had the most terrible row with Mother, who says I am to marry Major Stone, not you. She argues that he'll be a steadying influence on me, something I need more than anything else in this world. She didn't mention love once . . . oh, Toby you must save me before I succumb to palpitations of the most violent kind! Major Stone proposed to me and his hands—oh Toby, they were like sponge-cake, all squelchy and moist. You must come or I will surely die. Mother has locked me in my room, and our cook, who is my friend and ally, had to smuggle out this note.

"That does it!" Toby shouted, and crumpled the paper. "Dang it all, but we'll have to run away to Gretna Green tonight."

Almost too agitated to think clearly, Toby bundled clean shirts and neckcloths into a portmanteau. He weighed a heavy purse with guineas and decided it would have to last during the entire trip. He dashed off a note to his mother, sealed it, and placed it on his pillow. Then he donned his caped overcoat and sneaked down the back stairs.

It was an easy task to bribe one of the stablehands to

act as coachman for the journey. In total darkness, they hitched the Brownstoke traveling coach to four of the strongest horses and tried to leave the Brownstoke estate soundlessly. Somehow, he'd rescue Annabelle from her bleak tower and drive north at breakneck speed.

Drusilla Brownstoke was prostrate on her chaise longue, a cashmere shawl spread over her legs and a vinaigrette clutched in one trembling hand. Her red-rimmed eyes had the puffy look of long bouts of crying, and her pug nose had taken on a bold shade of red. Terence stared down at her, realizing she was not a sight to gladden the eye.

"You failed me," she said in dying tones. "You promised you would pay off that *hussy.*" Her voice rose to a wail. "You promised you would extricate Toby from her web." She dabbed at her eyes. "I'm ruined. I'll never be able to hold up my head again. What in the world shall I do now?"

"Are you sure they have eloped?" Terence saw his sister through a red haze of fury, a wrath that was directed toward the absent Miss Warwick.

Drusilla thrust a crumpled note into Terence's hand. "Read for yourself. I've read the message over and over, and there's no mistake."

Terence read aloud:

> "Most Beloved and Revered Mother. Don't fly into the Boughs and try to Avoid one of your Gruesome Turns as you read this. I have Eloped to Gretna Green with the Lady of my Heart. Don't Send Uncle T. after us. As you Peruse this, we will be Long Gone. Y'r Obedient Son, Tobias Brownstoke.

Terence frowned and clenched his fist around the missive. Damn his nephew, and double damn Miss

Warwick. She had schemed and convinced Toby to run away before it was too late.

"I'll show them!" Terence snarled and flung the ball of paper across the room. "It's early morning yet. They can't be that many hours ahead. On a fast horse, I shall catch up with them. Believe you me, Dru, I'll give Toby a tongue-lashing he won't soon forget."

"What are you going to do with Miss Warwick?" Drusilla asked feebly.

"I shall wring her miserable neck and send her off on one of the convict barges to the Colonies."

Drusilla's eyes widened in shock. "Such violence, Terence, but you do as you see fit. I'm too weak to accompany you and lend you my stalwart support." She clutched her vinaigrette bottle harder and narrowed her eyes. "I'll have some choice words for Miss Warwick when you return. That vile *creature* abducted poor Toby, who after all is still a minor."

Terence strode to the door. "I shall restore your precious son to you, never fear."

He rode all day, and most of the night. It was by luck and diligence that he, at dawn, came across the Brownstoke carriage at an inn north of London.

He roused an ostler to take care of his tired horse, then pounded on the door to alert the landlord.

Toby got a rude awakening five minutes later. Terence stared down at the younger man's sleep-heavy face in anger and suspicion. "Devil take it, Toby! Of all the havey-cavey things you've done in your life, this takes the grand prize."

"Don't shout at me," Toby said, bleary-eyed, and yawned hugely. " 'Tis too early in the morning."

Terence gripped his nephew's night shirt and twisted it under Toby's chin. "Where is she?"

Toby tried to shake off the punishing grip. "In the next room." He managed a sleepy smile. "We're pretending to be brother and sister traveling to a funeral."

"It might be yours," Terence said darkly, and stormed to the door. Carrying a lantern, he bounded into the annexing chamber and shook the figure huddled under the goose down cover.

"I shall string you up by your ears and skin you, Miss Warwick," he growled. He kept shaking her until a terrified face, edged by a lace-rimmed cap, emerged.

Shaken to the marrow, Terence could only stare at Annabelle Rushton's frightened eyes and pale face. "*You!* You aren't Miss Warwick." Deflated, he took a step back. After all, he'd sorely breached etiquette by accosting a female in her bedchamber.

"Lord P-Perth?" she asked in a quavering voice. "What's wrong? Is it my mother?" She clutched the edge of her cover to her chin. "Has she had a nervous fit? I knew eloping was a ramshackle thing to do, but there was no other way I could wed dear Toby. Mother wanted me to marry Major Stone, and I could not abide the thought of his clammy hands."

"Miss Rushton, are you telling me you're going to get shackled to my nephew?" Terence felt like a regular cod's head as he realized that no blame lay at Joanna Warwick's door.

"Oh, yes." Annabelle's voice grew stronger. "I would have liked to marry him in a romantic ceremony at the Hasselton church, but not with my mother breathing fire at the wedding. 'Tis Toby I love, always have."

Terence folded his arms across his chest and leaned against the door jamb. "I thought you weren't speaking to Toby. You gave him the cold shoulder at my ball."

"Well, that— You must admit that Toby has acted like a dimwit for the last three years."

Terence chuckled. "There's some truth to that, but I won't defame my nephew."

Toby stumbled over the threshold, dressed only in shirt and inexpressibles, hair standing up on his head. In Terence's eyes, he looked too young to think of wedlock, let alone eloping to Scotland. "Toby, I think this farce will have to end."

"Dearest Belle, don't listen to my uncle," Toby said with a dark look in Terence's direction. "I won't allow him to stop us from traveling to Gretna. I'll call him out if he as much as starts on one of his blistering lectures!"

Terence stared from one young person to the other and heaved a deep sigh. "Are you sure this is what you truly want to do?"

They nodded in unison. "We love each other," Toby said. "Ever since the day she put a toad under my shirt—we were seven and five at the time—I've had my eyes on her." He smiled mischievously. "After all, a female who dares to touch a toad is someone special, don't you think?"

Terence stifled a laugh. "You could be right." He nodded and apologized to Annabelle for intruding into her chamber, then pulled Toby out of the room and closed the door.

"Your mother will have a fit of the vapors when she hears about your sudden betrothal. Not that she has recovered from the one she fell into when she read your note."

Toby shrugged. " 'Tis only a matter of course. She has a fit every day. She will have to accept that I'm a grown man."

Terence was pleased to see the change in his ward, but it still bothered him that Toby had so recently been tied to Miss Warwick's apron strings. "I take it you have no feelings left for Miss Warwick?"

"She's a lady to her fingertips. At Miss Turnbull's birthday celebration, she pointed out that we would not suit. She gently reminded me that I still had unresolved feelings for Annabelle, then sent me away." He slapped his head with the flat of his hand. "I've been so blind! I thought I loved her, but I could never quite forget

Annabelle. It was gratifying to have Joanna's affection, and I mistook it for love. She never loved me, but she cherished my friendship. I shall apologize for my boorish behavior when we return to Hasselton, and I know she'll forgive me. She's the most kindhearted female I've ever met, honest and fair."

He stared hard at his uncle, and Terence had to look away as heat rose over his collar.

"Uncle Terence, *you* are taken with Miss Warwick. I can see it in your eyes."

"Gammon. 'Sfaith, I've naught but contempt for that woman—"

"—even though she's kind and honorable, sweet and beautiful?" Toby interrupted with a disdainful sneer. "Are you so blind that you can't see her qualities?" Toby stalked across the room, pushing his hands through his hair. "All these years I've looked up to you, Terence. You were my hero, someone who could not do any wrongful acts. I trusted your opinions and your fairness."

"Every human has his frailties," Terence said stiffly.

"That's a bag of moonshine. You're a fool if you can't see Joanna's true character. Are you so blinded by the gabble mongers that you've lost your sense of judgment? I swear Joanna was wrongfully accused." He flung out his arms in exasperation. "I maintain the blame lies wholly with Leslie Frinton."

Terence rubbed his jaw and stared thoughtfully at his nephew. "Is it your belief that Miss Warwick was *seduced* by Frinton, not the other way around?"

"I could drink poison to prove it! She's not capable of entrapment." Toby stopped before his uncle. "You'd be a fool not to offer for her. I've seen the smoldering looks you've sent in her direction. I was jealous, but I thought she would come to care for me in the end—which she didn't. Mayhap her heart was already engaged—to yours."

"Don't be daft, Toby. She's a . . . a . . ." He wanted to say hussy, but the word did not sit comfortably on his tongue any longer.

"Lady," Toby added with a mulish set of his jaw. "And if you don't mind, I need some sleep. Tomorrow is going to be a long day."

Terence tilted his head back and laughed. "Zounds! I think you're biting my head off." He strolled to the door. "However, it delights me to have gained a friend besides a nephew. I have every confidence in you, Toby. Promise me you'll make Annabelle happy."

"I promise," he said solemnly. Then he added, "You won't try to force us back to Sussex, will you?"

Terence shook his head. "No, I'll tell your mother I couldn't catch up with you."

Toby's face lit up and he gave Terence a bear hug. "You're a right one, Uncle T. I knew I could rely on you."

"You take care of Annabelle. I shall return to Sussex, but first I will stop in London to see my solicitor." Terence clapped his hat on his head and left.

Seventeen

"Look Joanna, we've received another invitation from Lord Perth," said Aunt Oddy as she peered at the gold-embossed note in her hand.

Joanna looked up from the ironmonger's bill beside her breakfast cup. "I will not attend." She stirred the steaming tea.

Aunt Oddy clucked her tongue and glanced at Joanna over the rims of her spectacles. "Of course you'll attend. You can't throw away this, possibly your last chance to reenter society. Lord Perth evidently is your champion who wants to see the past forgotten."

"You're a fool if you believe that, Aunt Oddy," Joanna said dryly. She hurriedly buttered a piece of golden toast and chewed one corner. She glanced repeatedly at the clock on top of the sideboard and tapped her slippered toe on the floor.

"Today is the day, Auntie. How will I ever convince Lord Thistlethorpe that I have no intention of marrying him?"

Oddy set down the invitation and toyed with her piece of toast. " 'Tis a most dreadful day. You look positively green around the gills, Jo. I wish—"

"You wish I had accepted Lord Perth's offer of money," Joanna filled in. "But no, I would never do such a low thing."

Oddy sighed heavily. "I might have wished that once. But really, long ago I hoped that your life had turned out differently, that your father hadn't been such a wastrel." Her eyes brimmed with compassion as she looked at her niece, and she nodded sagely. "You've had a heavy burden to bear."

Joanna's heart constricted with sadness and frustration. "Please don't rake up the past, Auntie. That will not improve our current situation."

Aunt Oddy's shoulders slumped. "What are we going to do? No one has asked for pianoforte lessons, and the flowers in the garden won't last forever."

Joanna clenched her jaw until it ached. "Mayhap I'll manage to strike some sort of a bargain with Lord Thistlethorpe."

"He's a most disagreeable man. My head is spinning with all that is going on." Oddy picked up the invitation with a listless hand. "Lord Perth has added a scrawl at the bottom that he expects us *both* to come. 'Twould be an opportunity to take our minds off our problems."

Joanna chewed on her lip as she cast about for ways to convince Lord Thistlethorpe to give her an extension on his loan. "When is the ball?"

"Next Saturday."

Joanna waited in suspense the entire day, but Lord Thistlethorpe did not arrive to pester her for a reply. She found his absence highly suspicious, but could not find a suitable reason for his change of plans. Perhaps he'd fallen ill and couldn't leave his house. Hope flared in her heart, but she felt guilty about wishing poor health upon her enemy.

As evening fell, she could finally relax. Her shoulders were iron rigid, and a headache gnawed at the base of her skull. Testy, and feeling sadly out of curl, she heaved herself up the stairs to her bedchamber.

During the week, her disposition brightened as Lord

Thistlethorpe had not darkened their doorstep. She asked Mrs. Dibble to find out in the village if there were any rumors about Thistlethorpe's health.

Mrs. Dibble reported that there was no gossip about the old rake. The village was agog with the rumor that Toby Brownstoke had abducted Annabelle Rushton and ridden off to Scotland with her slung over the pommel.

Joanna laughed. "That's ridiculous! Toby would not do such a ramshackle thing. I'm certain he brought his carriage and bore her off in style."

"Still, 'twas a scandalous thing to do. They say Mrs. Brownstoke is prostrate and in a haze of delirium. She got a letter from Toby explaining that he has married Miss Rushton, and that they are spending his birthday in the north. Such cold, uncharitable weather up north. I don't understand why—"

"Mrs. Brownstoke should be delighted at the turn of events. After all, her new daughter-in-law possesses an unsullied reputation. I wish them all the happiness." Joanna was glad that Toby had made the choice to swallow his pride and forgive Annabelle. "They were made for each other."

As the day of the ball came, Joanna felt almost hopeful enough to attend, but she changed her mind at the last moment. What if Thistlethorpe had been invited? He might corner her at some nook of the manor ballroom and demand her answer right then and there.

"You go alone," she said to Aunt Oddy, who was contemplating what to wear. "Or let McBorran escort you. He needs another chance to heal the breach with his grandson."

"That poor old man. He's been sadly drooping after young Perth snubbed him. I'd like to tweak the viscount's nose for such boorish behavior," Oddy said heatedly.

"Give him some more time. He might yet come about. Once he realizes that he can't change the past, and his pride is not at stake, he will accept Lord McBorran's apology."

Aunt Oddy held a taffeta dress in the empire style in front of her. She threw Joanna a keen glance. "Hmmm, seems like you've come to know Perth rather well."

"We didn't argue every time we met, but those peaceful encounters were few and far between. So much the better. But I know he has a good heart under his elegant coat."

Aunt Oddy fingered the pale blue material of the gown. "This might be just the thing for you. A few alterations and added embellishments, it'll be as good as new."

Joanna raised her chin into the air. "I'm not going, and that's the end of it."

She waved on the front step as her aunt went to the ball on Lord McBorran's arm. They giggled and chatted like children, and Joanna smiled as she listened. Too seldom did she hear her aunt's bell-like laugh, and she felt partly at fault. Oddy needed more friends.

Joanna went into the parlor and tucked her feet under her on the sofa. *Guy Mannering* lay unopened in her lap, but she would soon start reading. If only the strains of music didn't waft quite so clearly across the lawn. . . . If only she didn't picture the gold-and-cream ballroom with its gleaming parquet floor and glittering chandeliers. . . . If only—

A sharp knock sounded on the front door, interrupting her thoughts. Startled, she opened the door a crack. It was torn out of her hands and a male figure strode into the hallway. She gasped and cringed with fear until she recognized Lord Perth. He bristled with tension.

"My lord, what in the world? You scared me witless."

"I wrote specifically on the invitation that I expected

you at the ball," he shouted, and threw up his hands. "And you ignore my request. I find it very rude."

"You know the reason why I don't have any desire to attend the ball. Nothing has changed."

He gripped her wrist, and before she could protest, he'd pulled her up the stairs to her bedchamber.

"What in the world—?" Joanna cried as she stumbled over the threshold. "This is highly irregular—" Gaping, she watched as the viscount stalked to her clothespress and started to pull her gowns from their hooks. He tossed them into a heap onto her bed.

"Nothing but damned rags!" he bellowed when he'd tossed the last one on top of the rest.

"Lord Perth, you're acting in a demented fashion," Joanna scolded, but could barely keep herself from chuckling. He was a sight for sore eyes in his flawless cut-away coat and pristine linen. Black knee breeches molded his powerful thighs, and white silk stockings his calves. Joanna could not stop the warmth spreading through her as she watched his angry face. He cared. He'd missed her at the ball. "Your being here is a terrible breach of etiquette."

"I'll break every rule if that will suit my purpose." He lifted an outmoded white silk dress with a silver lace tunic that had a tarnished look. "Wear this. 'Twill have to do for now."

Their eyes clashed across the room. "You can't force me, milord," she said in a low voice.

"I can and I will . . . Joanna." He marched up to her and thrust the garment into her arms. "I'll give you twenty minutes to get ready."

They stared at each other for a long moment, and Joanna couldn't find the strength to argue further. She nodded as she twisted her mouth into a grimace. "Very well, if you want to make a laughingstock—"

"Don't say another word!" He went to the door.

"And don't call me 'milord' again. My name is Terence."

Joanna stared at his retreating back. Her head reeled with shock. She clutched the dress to her as if it were a life preserver. Looking into the mirror, she saw a pale face and a mass of untidy hair. She couldn't very well go to the ball, or could she? Did she dare? Perhaps she would be protected from malice if she entered on Perth's—Terence's—arm. "Don't be a ninny," she said to herself. "The gentry will never forget, and they won't let you forget."

Nevertheless, she went behind the painted screen in the corner and discarded her old gown and slippers. After a quick sponge wash, she pulled on the old white dress. A flood of memories washed over her. This was the gown she'd worn that miserable night with Leslie Frinton; she'd never worn it again, but perhaps it was time to bury the past.

The puff sleeves were slightly tight around her arms. Evidently her work in the garden had firmed up her muscles. She brushed her hair and wound it into a chignon at the back. For five minutes she hunted for gloves, fan, and slippers. She found a spray of pink silk flowers that she attached to her hair arrangement. She wound her mother's pearls around her neck, and a shawl embroidered with silver thread around her shoulders. With her heart hammering in her chest, she stepped downstairs.

He was waiting in the parlor, his face stiff with tension. He looked up immediately as she entered. His gaze raked over her like a hot breath.

"You look lovely, Joanna. In fact, I don't think I've ever seen you more enchanting."

"Flattery won't make a dent in my heart . . . Terence," she said, trying to still the quaver in her voice. "I don't understand why you insist that I take part in your schemes. Nothing good is bound to come of it."

He offered his arm. "Trust me . . . dearest Joanna."

Dearest? As he escorted her outside, Joanna could not remember a time when she'd been more intrigued. Without another word, she followed him to the waiting carriage.

The ballroom smelled of roses and elusive perfumes. The strains of violin and flute rose toward the molded plaster ceiling. The scents and sounds, the glitter of the assembled guests overwhelmed Joanna as she entered the room on the viscount's arm. She noticed the fluttering fans from the corner of her eye, the swirl of ballgowns in blues, pinks, and greens. Tiaras flashed fire and ostrich plumes dyed in various colors waved atop elaborate coiffures. Joanna searched for Aunt Oddy and Lord McBorran, but to her surprise, her gaze fell upon Lady Sally Jersey, one of the patronesses of Almack's in London. If Lady Jersey snubbed her . . . Joanna's cheeks grew hot with embarrassment. That would be the end of it—forever. She would be condemned from drawing rooms and ballrooms in every town of Britain.

Eyes from all sides bored into her, and the heat from the many candles made her feel faint. Condemning eyes, sly, curious, brooding, contemptuous, humorous, and compassionate eyes studied her.

"Keep on smiling," the viscount said from the side of his mouth. "I have everything under control." He led her to the spot where Lady Jersey was chattering with a group of dowagers.

"Sally, please meet my good friend and neighbor, Miss Warwick," Terence said in a firm voice. Joanna's attention snagged on the words "good friend" as she smiled at the bright-faced Lady Jersey. When had she ever been friends with Lord Perth?

"Miss Warwick, it has been a very long time," Lady Jersey said. "London hostesses have sorely missed you. I hear that you've taken up gardening on a grand scale, but that mustn't prevent you from paying your respects to your peers in London and elsewhere."

Joanna sagged with relief. Something must have happened to bring her back into the good graces of society. If Lady Jersey accepted her, everyone else would, too. "I have been extremely busy, but naturally I miss the Season sorely," she said, which was only half a lie. She didn't care overly for the dizzying round of balls and routs in the Metropolis. "And my friends."

The violins tuned into a waltz, and Joanna's spirits soared as the viscount bowed before her. "Would you care to dance with me, Joanna?" He looked deeply into her eyes, and she noticed the half-smile lurking on his lips.

"I would be honored," she murmured, and let him lead her onto the floor. Other couples swirled to the music around them, but Joanna was only aware of Terence's dark eyes and the stubborn slant of his jaw. He smelled of sandalwood and leather, and she couldn't breathe deeply enough to print an indelible memory on her heart. Her breath came in small gasps as happiness sought to choke her. He whirled her around the floor, and she floated in his arms, her feet barely touching the polished parquet. Among so many of his compelling, if sometimes annoying, traits—flamboyance, single-mindedness, ruthlessness, rashness—he was an expert dancer. She'd never been swept around in such abandon, and she caressed his firm shoulder. He squeezed her hand in his and twirled her out onto the terrace.

Panting, they leaned against the balustrade. The sky was a brilliant canopy of black velvet and diamonds. Joanna pressed her hands to her flushed cheeks and wondered if one could die from too much happiness.

"I'd like to kiss you my dearest, but there is something I need to show you first. Come." He took her hand and pulled her along the terrace.

"Should I trust you?" she asked in a suspicious voice. "What deviousness will I have to face now?"

He laughed. "None. Our days of exchanging and parrying verbal thrusts are over. Only words of love will be spoken from now on."

She gasped, shocked at his revelation. A delicious warmth spread through her at the thought of hearing him whisper endearments into her ears.

He escorted her into the brightly lit library, and when Joanna's eyes had adjusted, she came face to face with a sullen-faced Leslie Frinton sitting in a leather wing chair. He still looked devilishly handsome with his dark Byron curls, sallow complexion, and hooked nose. His eyes still had a brooding quality that might easily pull at female heartstrings. It had at hers. He rose slowly.

"Leslie! What are you doing here?" Joanna croaked. She glanced wildly at Terence, and noticed her aunt sitting in one of the armchairs fanning herself frantically.

"Frinton told the whole story to Lady Jersey," Terence explained. He stepped up to the younger man and pushed a long finger into Leslie's chest. "You will now apologize for the pain you caused Miss Warwick, and you will do it on your knees."

Leslie scowled, but the viscount clamped his hand on Leslie's shoulder and pushed him down.

Confused, Joanna watched. "I don't understand," she whispered to Terence, but he only shook his head and gazed at her in encouragement. He squeezed her hand and pushed the toe of his evening shoe into Leslie's side.

"Speak up, Frinton, or you will not get off as easily. I shall see you persecuted."

Leslie licked his lips and gripped one of Joanna's hands. "Joanna, you must forgive me. I was very wrong to use you in such a despicable manner. It was my fault that you were shunned by everyone and had to rusticate in the country. Hoping that my fiancée would jilt me, I lured you into that dark room to seduce you." He gave a snort. "It worked beyond my wildest hope. An embrace, a bare breast—very effective."

Joanna swallowed convulsively. Her head spun, and the whole world seemed to have tilted sideways. Angry, she snatched her hand from his moist grip. "Don't touch me!"

"Say that you forgive me."

"Why should I?" Joanna looked uncertainly from Aunt Oddy's excited face to Terence's. He nodded imperceptibly. She was swimming in a sea of indecision, but his nod was a buoy she could cling to, a gesture she had to trust.

"Very well, I don't really want to, but I forgive you for breaking my heart, and destroying my life, Leslie. Now get up from that ridiculous position."

He obeyed with alacrity. Joanna studied his face and wondered how she'd ever been so infatuated with the man. He was vain—a fop, really. Next to Terence, he looked like a veritable milksop.

She fought an urge to laugh out loud. "Can someone explain this?" she asked, and glanced in Aunt Oddy's direction.

Oddy's eyes glowed with relief and delight. "Oh, Joanna, you won't believe this, but Lord Thistlethorpe *paid* Mr. Frinton to ruin you. Thistlethorpe wanted you for himself, and when your father lost everything, Thistlethorpe was more than eager to step in and alleviate our burdens. If he hadn't been married at the time, he would have insisted that you wed him on the spot."

"Thistlethorpe? Well, I should have known. He was forever fawning over me when I grew up." Joanna quelled her rising anger. "But that he would pay—?" She gazed in wonder at Leslie Frinton. "Is it the truth?"

He nodded coolly. "I needed the money. Am I free to

go now?" he asked, and the viscount pushed him toward the door.

"Proceed! And don't show your phiz here again, or I will have to beat you to an inch of your life."

Joanna watched her erstwhile beau leave the room, his back stiff with effrontery.

Aunt Oddy rose from her chair and wound her arm around Joanna's waist. "Lord Perth hasn't told the entire story. Come and sit with me, Jo."

They sat close together on the sofa, and Terence handed them each a snifter of brandy. "Drink this." She obeyed, and he hitched his hip onto the edge of his desk and dangled a leg. The brandy sent a burning ribbon to her stomach and spread warmth throughout her body.

She met Terence's unflinching, admiring stare, and she felt even warmer. He began, "I managed to overtake Toby on the Great North Road. I discovered that Annabelle would be a good wife to Toby, and vice versa, so I let them go." He held a finger to his lips. "You won't tell Dru, will you, Joanna?"

She shook her head, laughter bubbling in her throat. "I might be to blame for their rash action. I sent Toby away so that he could make peace with Annabelle."

The viscount looked pleased and heaved a deep sigh. "I discovered from Toby that he'd started to investigate the background of Frinton. I went to my solicitor and asked him to learn more. It turned out that Frinton is a fortune hunter, a hanger-on with some connections in the upper echelons. That's how he came to be introduced to all the debutantes during the Season the year you came out. He got engaged to a duke's daughter, but later discovered that the duke would not put a single groat into Frinton's pocket if he married the daughter. Evidently, the young lady was deeply infatuated with Frinton and wouldn't give him up. Thistlethorpe approached him with an offer of money to ruin you,

Joanna. Frinton saw the opportunity to make his fiancée jilt him if he seduced another woman. That lady was you."

"A scurvy snake," Oddy said with a tremble in her voice. "He ought to be boiled in oil."

The viscount chuckled. "Aptly put, Miss Turnbull. He's a scoundrel of the worst kind."

"But how did you force Frinton to speak up and apologize?" Joanna asked.

"My solicitor found out that Frinton had run through the money that Thistlethorpe gave him and chalked up large gambling debts." Terence gave her a keen stare. "I offered to pay them in lieu of a confession to Lady Jersey and your aunt. Five thousand pounds."

Joanna gasped. "That's what you offered me—"

"I know. I was doomed to lose that sum one way or the other," he said ruefully. "So I paid Frinton, and he told the truth. His current fiancée found out from my solicitor what kind of man Frinton is. She isn't likely to marry him now." He took a sip of brandy. "Frinton will probably live in obscurity from now on. When this story travels around, he'll be cut dead by his peers. Let him live with the kind of humiliation you had to experience in Hasselton."

Joanna drank some more brandy and the room soon took on a rosy glow. "You did all this for . . . me?"

The viscount gave a devilish smile. "Clever of me, wasn't it? Anyway, I ultimately benefit from it as well." He reached over the desk and pulled out the middle drawer. His hand returned with a stiff folded paper in his hand. He gave it to Joanna, who immediately recognized her promissory note to Lord Thistlethorpe. She held it gingerly between thumb and forefinger. "You managed to get this . . . how?"

The viscount shrugged, another smile raising the corners of his lips. "Well, you know he's an inveterate gambler."

She nodded vigorously. "Why, yes, my father lost prodigious amounts of money to Thistlethorpe. It was painful to watch." She lowered her gaze as a moment of sadness pierced her happiness.

"Thistlethorpe owes you more than an apology, but I squashed his fondest wish, to make you his bride."

"We were fortunate that he was still married when Joanna got the loan, or else—" said Aunt Oddy. "I think he poisoned his last wife, and I worried so that Joanna would go the same way. Thank God that she's so stubborn." Aunt Oddy snatched the promissory note from Joanna and tore it in tiny pieces. She got up and tossed them into the ashes in the fireplace, then smiled benignly at the viscount.

"You've shown yourself in fine fettle, milord. If only you could find it in your heart to forgive your grandfather, I would look even more favorably upon you." She patted Joanna's arm. "I'll leave you alone for five minutes, then you must join the ball. Everyone will be eager to make amends now that Sally Jersey gave you her blessing."

Joanna's heartbeat escalated alarmingly as her aunt left her alone with the viscount. He took her hand and led her out onto the terrace. She held her breath as he slowly pulled her into his arms. A faintness came over her as he lowered his mouth to hers. At first their lips touched like butterfly wings, nudging, tasting, familiarizing themselves. The kiss deepened to sweep a storm of sensations through Joanna's body. His tongue was silky soft, yet demanding her fiery response, her acceptance. Weak-kneed, she let him lift her off her feet and press her full-length to himself. When his grip loosened, all the bones in her body had suddenly melted, and she could barely stand.

"I love you," he whispered into her hair. "I think I've loved you since the day you told me to take my money and drown myself. I was jealous of Toby, so jealous.

But I couldn't admit my feelings for you, not even to myself. That was cowardly. I was too stubborn to accept the truth."

"What changed that?" Joanna asked when she could find her voice.

"You . . . at the market, when I realized I had to have you or die with disappointment. When I found Toby, he pointed out all my shortcomings, and I actually *listened*. Sometimes he's wiser than I am, much more so." His voice lowered with embarrassment. "You know, I would have used Thistlethorpe's promissory note to force you away from Toby, but I never had to resort to such vile tactics."

She threaded her fingers through his hair. "It would not have worked. I can be just as stubborn as you, or worse." She sighed with contentment. "But, I think it's clear that you've swallowed your stubborn pride, at last."

"Do you love me, Joanna?" he asked, his voice suspiciously fragile. He nuzzled her nose with his. "Say that you do."

She nodded. "Yes, I love you. Very much."

"Will you do me the honor of becoming my wife?"

"Yes . . . maybe."

"I can't promise that I'll never shout at you, but I promise to always cherish you even when you get on your high horse."

"Very comforting thought," Joanna said, laughing. "However, there is one thing you have to do before I consent."

His eyes widened in question.

"You have to heal the breach with Lord McBorran."

He pulled away with a burst of agitation. "I can't do that!"

She took his hand in a firm grip. "Yes, you can. That is, if you still want to bring me to the altar."

He flung out his arms. "Very well, I'll talk to him,

but I can't promise I'll surrender! Where's that old man?"

"I thought I spied him in one of the corners, all alone."

Joanna waited with Terence as a footman went in search of Lord McBorran and Oddy. The couple entered five minutes later, arm in arm. Joanna could see the light of battle in Aunt Oddy's eyes, and she smiled. McBorran had staunch support in his difficult moment.

A bent and tired McBorran stepped up to Terence and looked deeply into his grandson's eyes. With a face full of contrition, the old man quavered, "I love you, Terence."

Joanna's eyes filled with tears as she watched the old earl bare his soul. He seemed so frail that a gust of wind might blow him away.

"I've always loved you, grandson, but I have never been a good example to you. In fact, I've scorned all that is good in this world and lived a worthless life. It took me sixty years to realize that. I'm so sorry that I ruined your life in the process. If I could make amends for the years you had to spend abroad, I would dearly like to do so."

Silence hung heavy in the room, and Aunt Oddy squared her shoulders as if ready to do battle. Joanna squeezed Terence's arm.

"Very well, Grandfather," he said at last. "Since this is a night to bury the past, let bygones be bygones. My years in India were not totally wasted." He gave a lop-sided grin. "At least I got a pet monkey." He held out his hand to his grandfather, but got a bear hug. "But I'd like to speak with you alone," he said into the old man's shoulder.

Joanna urged Aunt Oddy out onto the terrace, leaving the two men behind.

Terence led his grandfather to the nearest sofa and helped him to sit down. He pulled up a chair and sat next to McBorran. "I can forgive you for your gambling and your whoring, Grandsire, but I have difficulty accepting that you supported my mother when she left the family. Why didn't you see to it that she lived a decent life?"

McBorran's shoulders sagged as he stared into the ashes in the fireplace. "You never understood this, but your father was a rather spoiled and violent man. He beat your mother repeatedly, and when she finally found the courage to leave and seek a better life, I assisted her. I didn't know, however, that she had run off with one of the grooms. She lived in squalor in London after he left her, and she was too proud to take my money." He slanted a shrewd glance at Terence. "You got your mulishness from her." He sighed. "I discovered that she was afflicted with consumption, and she continually refused my offers of help. I even got a physician to visit her, and she threw him out."

Terence felt the old pain well up in his chest, the pain of betrayal. "I thought she had a shameful disease. That's what Father implied."

"No . . . she never had. I would have aided her even as she became an outcast for running away with the stable groom, but she abhorred me as much as she abhorred your father." He leaned over the armrest and clutched Terence's arm. "You must forgive her and go on with your life. If my son—your father—had not mistreated her, she might still be with us. The fault lies with me, who spoiled my only son until he could think of no one but himself."

Terence felt the relief of a heavy burden being lifted from his shoulders. He understood the truth now, understood that the explanations with which his father had filled his ears were nothing but angry recriminations against someone who had thwarted him. Somehow the haze of anger that had filled his mind for so long had dissolved with the truth, and he felt at peace.

"You remember that, Terence, and always treat Joanna with respect. Cherish her forever."

Joanna entered, and she had evidently overheard. "I like those words, Lord McBorran."

"I promise," Terence said quietly.

Everyone laughed, and Aunt Oddy gave an audible sigh of relief. McBorran beamed like a thousand candles.

"We've something to tell you," Terence said with a hitch in his voice. He looked at Joanna with love, and her eyes brimmed over with happy tears.

"Joanna has promised to become my wife. I'm the luckiest man in the world."

Joanna laughed and held up her finger. "Not so fast, my lord. You have yet to promise that you'll push my wheelbarrow in the garden from now on."

The viscount gave a howl of laughter and swung her around by the waist. "You drive a hard bargain."

"I learned it doesn't pay to be naive." She looked down at his adoring face.

"I will push your wheelbarrow now and—forever."